Makin' Happy

a novel by

Niki Kendall

authorHOUSE®

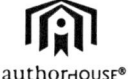

AuthorHouse™
1663 Liberty Drive, Suite 200
Bloomington, IN 47403
www.authorhouse.com
Phone: 1-800-839-8640

© 2009 Niki Kendall. All rights reserved.

No part of this book may be reproduced, stored in a retrieval system, or transmitted by any means without the written permission of the author.

First published by AuthorHouse 3/13/2009

ISBN: 978-1-4389-5218-5 (sc)

Library of Congress Control Number: 2009900706

Printed in the United States of America
Bloomington, Indiana

This book is printed on acid-free paper.

This is dedicated to my dear
friend and guardian angel,
Sharon Rose Hobbs Bell

Earth certainly is not
the same without you.

I love you and miss you woman!

ACKNOWLEDGEMENTS

First and foremost I would like to thank the goddess who rules my universe, my daughter and my reason for living Kyrie. Thank you for saving my life. Your brilliance and light makes the world a much more beautiful place.

Mom and Dad, you have been a constant support in my life. I could not begin to thank you enough. Mom, you manage to make this world brighter.

My cousin Janeeda Fernandez, you are like the sister I never had. Thank you for your amazing phone calls, your sisterhood and for lending your brilliant artwork to this labor of love.

My oldest and dearest friend Maureen Walsh, thank you for coming back into my life and making me remember the fabulousness of us. You are so beautiful and like a fairy, you wave your magic wand and sprinkle a little pixie dust and make this world and many people in it, more beautiful.

Robin Strand, my sister in weathering storms how can I thank you for the endless pep talks and "that a girl's"? Your friendship is proof that beautiful things can come from less than beautiful circumstances. Thank you for lending your insight to this project and for encouraging me to finish.

All of the sister-girlfriends and students who touched my life and inspired me, I thank you.

Last but certainly not least, Don Cush, thank you for showing me what a loving and supportive relationship looks like.

All the musicians who created music that kept me going through this project and inspired me to set the moods of every chapter. Especially INXS, who provided the soundtrack to some of the most important moments in my life and set the pace for every chapter of this book.

CONTENTS

Chapter One	Dancing on the Jetty	1
Chapter Two	"It's" the one thing	19
Chapter Three	Original Sin	33
Chapter Four	Don't Change	47
Chapter Five	New Sensation	57
Chapter Six	The Swing	67
Chapter Seven	By My Side	87
Chapter Eight	Bitter Tears	105
Chapter Nine	Never Tear Us Apart	119
Chapter Ten	Mystify Me	131

CHAPTER ONE

Dancing on the Jetty

WATCH THE WORLD ARGUE. ARGUE WITH YOURSELF,
WHO'S GONNA TEACH ME PEACE AND HAPPINESS?

Asia and Rebecca Blake breathed a sigh of relief when the car was finally parked on the ferry.

"Mom, let's go up on deck, its beautiful this time of day." Asia was right. It was a hazy August evening and the sun was just about to set, leaving its orange reflection on the water. When they arrived to the upper deck, Rebecca took a deep breath and closed her eyes. She had not been to Martha's Vineyard since Asia was a teenager. Now she's a grown woman. Rebecca opened her eyes and fastened them on Asia. *Twenty-seven*, she said to herself, *my baby is the same age as me when I had her.*

"Mom, what's wrong?"

"Nothing. I'm just enjoying this and I'm glad you talked me into coming." Rebecca was a beautiful woman; her skin was fair, a bit yellow, in need of some sun. Her hair was jet black with strands of gray at the temples. She smiled warmly and looked at Asia.

"Well I'm glad that you came, especially on such short notice. I could really use your help since Devin and I split and Sam had to cancel at the last minute." Asia paused, "I just hope you don't mind this being sort of a working vacation."

"I'm just glad to get away from the office."

"Terrific, I've got some killer plans, and with yours and Uncle Al's money and my ideas, the house is going to be all of that."

"How did I know that I'd wind up footing the bill for your so-called business venture?"

"Trust me Ma, once the house is freshened up, we can rent it out the weeks that we won't be there and you will soon see a return on your investment."

"This is good for me, we don't get to spend much time together and I've got some great ideas of my own for sprucing up the place."

"Good. Besides, you are not only excellent company; you are amazing with a paintbrush. But Ma, are you sure you're going to be okay? I mean, I know you have not been to stay in the house since Grandpa died in it years ago." Asia felt awkward asking her mother about her avoiding the Vineyard and her reason behind it. She knew that her mother was not the type to get emotionally bent out of shape over the death of a loved one, but her father and that house were important fixtures in her life. Rebecca had worked and struggled to make her father proud. She was comforted by the fact that he died knowing that she was successful and able to take care of herself and her family.

"Trust me I'm fine. Not to change the subject but being that you did bring him up, whatever happened between you and Devin?"

Asia flashed a frustrated grin, "It was like...he crowded me Ma, ya know? I mean he just wasn't for me."

"Sure, you know I always felt that way about him."

"He really stifled my creativity. He was not supportive of me or my work at all."

"Not to say I told you so, but I must say that I was surprised that you both stayed together for so long."

"Yeah, eleven months wasted. But I found myself accepting shit from him that I wouldn't ordinarily tolerate. All the while I was saying to myself 'Relationships are all about compromise, and if you want it, you've got to deal with him.' Then one day I realized that was all a bunch of crap society drills into women so we will put up with all of the shit men dish out. I decided not to accept anything from him that made me uncomfortable or unhappy. Like that time he read my diary and then confronted me on issues that concerned him, as if I should be embarrassed by my past or explain to him the reason why I did things that I did, before I even met him."

"Oh yes, I remember that well. I must say I was surprised that you forgave him and blown away that you took him back after that."

"Well if you were so blown away, how come you never said anything?"

"Asia, if I spoke out on everything you did that blew me away, I'd never shut up. You know me well enough to know that I believe that this is your life, and you have got to make your own decisions, and not base that decision on what I think is right or wrong."

"That's cool, that's why I love you so much, and I swear I'm lucky to have you, now if only I could get Daddy to see things your way."

"Are you kidding? Your father still thinks that you are twelve years old, forget about it."

They both chuckled. Asia looked out to the water and took a deep breath of the warm air. She shut her eyes and listened to the clanking of the buoys that guided the ships. She wished that her heart had something like that to follow. Love to Asia was almost a blinding thing. It was like walking through an unfamiliar house in the dark, once you learn exactly how to move around, you take advantage and get lazy. The care and excitement that overwhelms you in the beginning are replaced with contempt and disrespect. She opened her eyes and surveyed the deck. It seemed as if everyone was paired up and in love. It was times like this when she missed Devin.

Oak Bluffs was jammed as usual. Asia and Rebecca stopped at the little seafood take-out off of Circuit Avenue for a pint of shrimp and clams to take to the house.

"Oh Ma, before we go to the house, I'm gonna run to the liquor store, I have a taste for a cold beer with dinner. Do you want anything?"

"No I'm just going to start on a shrimp or two, don't take too long. Better yet, get me a diet soda please."

Asia walked into the store smiling at a familiar looking couple exiting the store. She headed toward the beer, hoping to find Beck's Light. It was nowhere in sight, as she turned around to ask the boy behind the counter, she bumped into Timmy Moses reaching to tap her on her shoulder.

"Hey stranger." He smiled.

"Timmy Moses, talk about a blast from the past! What's going on?" Asia reached to hug him.

"Not much babe, damn it has been a long time." He hugged her back.

"So are you still Dee Jaying at Visage?"

"No, I'm managing a restaurant in Patterson now. So what are you up to? I still catch your show every now and then."

"Well I'm still at the station, but I'm still writing. I'm trying to get my second book published. So, are you vacationing alone or with a significant other?" Asia winked at him.

"I'm here with my boy Rae, you know Rae don't you?"

"No I don't believe..."

"Yo Tim, do we want plain or Citron?" Rae came walking toward them holding two bottles of Absolute Vodka.

"Rae, this is Asia Blake, she's an old buddy of mine from Jersey."

"The Asia Blake?" Rae put a bottle under his arm and extended his right hand. "From WBRB New York?"

"Yes, the one and only. How ya doin' Rae, it's nice to meet you." Asia shook his hand.

"Hey, you sound even better in person, I listen to you often."

Asia felt like she was blushing, if she were light-skinned, it would have been a dead giveaway. "Thank you. Wait, you look awfully familiar. Oh yeah, your Doctor Gaymon on that Soap Opera."

"That's me. Rae Underhill and the pleasure is all mine."

"That's a great show; I watch it all the time." She lied.

Timmy cut in. "Well now that we've established mutual fan clubs, what's up for tonight?"

"My Mom and I are going back to the house for dinner. Why, what's going on?"

"Well Peter Sharpe is having a little party tonight at his father's place, why don't you come over, hey bring your mother, there's gonna be some old heads out tonight too." Timmy flashed his winning smile. Rae just silently stared at Asia, as if he were studying her every move.

"Over on Carole right?"

"You bet. Asia, how's my girl Cymone doing?"

"She's doing quite well, you know she's teaching in East Orange and working on her Master's Degree. She was going to join me but she took Brianna down to Atlanta to see her father."

"So did they ever get married?"

"Nope. Actually he's living with someone else, so she's quite single. Are ya still interested?"

"Hell yeah. Listen we've gotta run, I'll get with you later on Cymone."

"It was nice meeting you Asia." Rae grabbed her hand and firmly shook it. "I hope to see you later on this evening."

Asia smiled and felt a flutter in her stomach, "I'm sure we'll meet again."

Driving to the house Asia silently observed her mother's shock at how crowded the island had become. Glancing out into the ocean Asia thought of Rae. *He was kind of cute,* she thought to herself, *but he's not my type.* He was very fair skinned with freckles, he reminded her of her grandfather. He was also a bit shorter than the type she usually went for. He was stocky, built like a football player; she preferred the basketball player types with dark skin. Nonetheless, she felt something when he looked at her.

After eating, Asia was ready to shower and hit the street. Rebecca was tired, so she turned in. Asia raced out of the shower and threw on an oversized poet shirt and a black mini skirt and clogs. She let down her long curly brown hair and dabbed on a touch of red lipstick.

She jumped into the jeep and put in the reggae tape she dubbed from her little brother Josh. The night was perfect for a party. She got to Peter's house and parked next to Timmy's BMW. She walked toward the crowd, wearing a forced smile, speaking to people whose names had long been forgotten.

Rae hugged her from behind. "Let me get you a cocktail." He whispered in her ear.

"Sure." She smiled and followed him to the bar.

He waved over the bartender, and then turned to Asia. "What would you like?"

"White Zinfandel, please." She pulled herself up onto a barstool and waved to an acquaintance from Jersey.

"Corona with a shot of tequila and a White Zinfandel please." He turned back to Asia and smiled. "So you come here often?"

"I try to come up every summer, if only for a weekend. This trip is business though. I'm here to do some redecorating on our house. What about you?"

"I have not been here since I was in high school. My family used to come up every summer.

"Do you own or rent?"

"Borrow, the place belongs to my Dad's best friend."

Asia and Rae talked for two hours. They realized that they had met over ten years ago at a Jack and Jill convention. After several drinks, the conversation shifted.

Rae looked suddenly serious, paused for a moment then blurted out "You look prettier than your voice."

"Thanks...I think." She chuckled.

"Oh, it's definitely a compliment, I mean, you have an amazing voice but, you are so beautiful."

Asia blushed. "Listen, I have a confession to make."

"Already - wow."

"I... I um, I really don't watch your show all the time."

"I kind of figured that." He smiled and ran his hands over his smooth baldhead; Asia noticed this was sort of a nervous habit of his.

"May I?" She asked, reaching her hand out to touch his head. "I mean you keep touching it, now you've got me curious as to how it feels."

"Sure."

"Oh my, it is so soft and fuzzy."

Rae pulled back abruptly and reached for his pager on his belt loop. He squinted to read the message then shook his head in aggravation.

"Is that your wife looking for you?" She asked jokingly.

"Why do you ask?" He sounded serious.

Asia hesitated to answer. *Oh shit don't tell me this guy is married!* She thought to herself. She reached down and grabbed his left hand. *No ring. Cool. But wait, shit, a tan line.*

"All right buddy, come clean, are you married or what?"

He looked at her, amazed deciding if he was going to lie to her or not. "Yes," he said bluntly, "I'm married."

"For how long?"

"Nine months."

"Kids?"

"Well, we got married because she was pregnant, but she lost the baby, so no, no kids."

"I'm sorry. Is she here?"

"No, she's in New York pissed off with me because I'm here with Timmy. She hates him."

"Well, I can't blame her. If Timmy was my husband's best friend, I'd hate him too."

"Why?" Rae chuckled.

"Because Timmy is, don't get me wrong, he's a sweetie, but he's a Ho."

"Damn, you must know him well." Rae looked away then peered deeply into Asia's eyes. "How do you feel about married men?"

Asia felt excited; he was after all quite sexy. "I don't feel much for men these days, married or otherwise."

"Why is that?"

"Well no offense, but men, to me, were sent here to get on women's nerves, for the most part. From my past experiences, men have just stifled my creativity."

"How so?"

"Well, I'm working on a book; I'm a writer, I Dee Jay to support my work. Anyway, while I was working on my Master's Degree, my old boyfriend Greg read my thesis. When he finished it I told him that my dream was to get a Doctorate in Women's Studies. And do you know what this asshole said to me?"

Rae hung on her every word. "No, what did he say?"

He said 'Asia, if you want to get a degree in Women's studies, I suggest you get married and have a couple of kids, so you will really know what it means to be a woman.' "

"Wow, he was an asshole."

"Exactly. I couldn't believe that he would fix his lips to say some shit like that to me, as if my existence as a woman is validated and complete once I hitch myself to a man and bear children."

"Yes, I see your point, but you know all men are not..."

"Yeah, I know but that just set me off. And I thought I was going to marry this man."

"So what happened between you two?"

I served him his walking papers. I decided it was better to be alone than stay with someone who devalues my work, my beliefs and my gender."

Makin' Happy

"Not only all that beauty but brains to boot. Let's go for a walk."

"Sure." He held her hand and led her down a pathway to a secluded wooded area. In the center of the lot, there was a gazebo.

Asia questioned herself. *Why am I spending time with him still?* They talked for five hours. *He's not my type, even though he is sexy as hell. What am I talking about? He's married.* But she continued to enjoy his company. He was witty and a delightful conversationalist, that was such a hard thing to come by. She realized that she enjoyed him so much because of the simple things many men don't do. He read books; he was able to recite poetry not just lyrics from a song. He was smart, and most of all a feminist. He was the first black male Asia met who agreed with her whole heartedly that John Singleton portrayed sickening images of women in his films. And that Desire Washington wasn't wrong for being in Mike Tyson's room after midnight. He agreed that when a woman said 'no' it meant just that. Asia realized that his mother had done a good job with him - he and his three sisters.

As they walked and talked, the romantic vibes surrounding her consumed Asia. Before she knew it, their lips were lightly touching; the chaste and sterile kisses ended up in a passionate kiss and embrace. Asia pulled away suddenly.

"Rae, I'd better go, I don't know what I'm doing here and I don't know why I'm doing this."

"Okay, but let me walk you to your car."

"Thanks."

As they walked to the car, the silence and tension was thick. Asia had a strict policy on married men, to leave them alone. She always feared that if she got involved with a married man, once she got married, she'd be cursed. It would be fate that her husband would cheat on her. As they approached the house, Asia wondered, *why him? Why do I like him? He's charming, witty, handsome, well known, respectful-* and MARRIED.

"Well here you are." Rae whispered. He too was a bundle of unspoken emotions. *Why her?* He thought to himself. *Why do I like her? She's the first woman I've met in a long time that I can relate to. She's not phony like so many of these other women. She's so smart. So real.*

"Thank you." Asia stuck out her hand to shake his.

He took her hand and whispered, "Will I see you back home?"

All of her wanted to scream 'no', but "Yes." flowed from her lips.

Asia went straight to bed but couldn't sleep. She was haunted by a conversation with her grandmother about how young people have no values.

"Life means nothing," Mother Blake squealed. "Why do these young people run around here and shoot each other down?"

Asia took a deep breath, "Well Nana, to them, life has little value, a gold watch or a pair of sneakers means more than a human life."

"And marriage," Mother Blake sighed and softly said, "it means nothing."

The word nothing echoed in Asia's head. She jumped up from bed and heard the television coming from the family room. She glanced at the alarm clock; it was 5:30 AM. *What is she doing?* Asia wondered.

Asia slipped on her robe and limped into the family room, everything was still draped in white sheets. Rebecca was sitting on the sofa playing solitaire on the lap top computer, listening to CNN and eating M&M's.

"Ma, what's up, insomnia again?"

"Of course. How was the party?"

"It was good. I saw some people I have not seen in years." Asia wanted to tell her about Rae, but was paralyzed by the thought. *Yeah we're close and all but she'd be pissed if she knew I kissed a married man tonight.* "Hey, do you wanna go to the beach tomorrow after we paint?"

"Oh an evening beach run?" Rebecca sounded excited. "God we haven't done that since Josh was little. Love to."

Her friends thought it was strange but Asia's mother loved to take the kids to the beach at night. It was more tranquil, peaceful, and when it was really hot, the water felt warm, like a bath.

"It's inevitable; you're becoming your mother."

"Scary isn't it?" Asia shook her head.

"Actually, I kind of like it. When you were a kid, you tried so hard to be different from me because you thought I was weird. You wanted me to be like your friend's moms." She popped a handful of M&M's in her mouth, "Now look at ya, we are more alike than ever."

"That's true. I couldn't understand why you weren't so social. You hated the Jack and Jill meetings, you never hung out at the club playing tennis and having your nails done, you'd rather hang out at Bloomie's with me. And you traded in the Links meetings so we could learn how to throw pots." Asia grabbed some M&M's and kissed her mother on top of her head, "Yeah, you're pretty cool."

"I knew you'd come around and realize that it was more important to me to spend quality time with you, rather than sit around and pretend that I have nothing better to do with my time. And to walk into a room with a bunch of ladies and act like I'm so important, is not my thing. Hell, I believe that a lot of your friend's mothers are treated like shit at home and at work so, when they do get involved in these organizations to gossip and throw their weight around, thinking that makes them important. When it's time for work to be done I'm there, otherwise, don't hassle me with petty bullshit."

"I hear ya Ma. Listen I'm going to sleep I'll see ya in a bit."

Gershwin blasting on the radio awakened Asia. She walked into the family room and found Rebecca on a ladder painting away.

"Throw on your handy man specials; I could use your help."

Asia shook her head, "Ma, you are too much. I'll be right back."

Rebecca and Asia painted all day. Rebecca compromised and let Asia play a few Ziggy and Bob Marley tapes, and Asia put up with the show tunes. They finished the family room, two bathrooms, and the living room where Devin had left off.

Asia and Rebecca had been invited to Mrs. Thomas' house for desert. Mrs. Thomas and Mother Blake, Asia's grandmother, were Bridge partners for over four decades. Asia recalled the first time she went with Mother Blake to Mrs. Thomas' house on the Vineyard for Bridge night. All Asia wanted to do was go hang on Circuit Avenue with Alicia, her buddy from DC. There were these two cuties from Michigan they met at the Inkwell.

"But Nana, can't I just walk to Circuit Ave? All my friends will be there" Asia whined.

"Sweetie, your mother sent you here for me to watch you, and that is what I'm going to do. Now sit back and take notes."

"Yes Grandmother."

Asia unenthusiastically watched four silver haired ladies compete in a ruthless game of Bridge. She laughed off her anger listening to them talk about various folks on the island. Asia was entertained and fortunate to be in a roomful of black women with knowledge and experience on their side.

The memory faded.

"Asia, let's call it a day, go get a bite to eat and take some ice cream to Mrs. Thomas' house."

"Okay Ma, why don't you hop in the shower, I just want to finish this spot. Before you go could you grab me a beer please?"

"Sure."

Asia looked out the window and saw Timmy's BMW parked across the street, the top was down and someone was sitting in the driver side. She squinted and realized that it was Rae. *What the fuck?* She thought to herself as she climbed down the ladder. When he realized that she had spotted him, he motioned for her to come outside.

"Here's your beer, I'm off."

"Thanks ma." Asia took the beer from her mother's hand, pulled her painters cap on backwards and walked out the door squinting.

"Hey, I hope you don't mind but I was uh," Rae pulled his full body up and sat on the top of the front seat. "I was nowhere near your neighborhood, so I decided to drop by." He leaned over to kiss her and she pulled away and looked toward her house. She saw Rebecca walk away from the window.

"How did you find out where I lived?"

"Timmy." He pointed to her beer, "May I?"

"Sure. Oh yeah, I forgot. So what's up?"

"If you want me to leave, I'll go. But I just wanted to see you again. I had to..."

She cut him off "I'm flattered, really."

He leaned over and gently kissed her.

"Rae," Asia's pulse was racing, he was an awesome kisser. "You are married, I can't do this." And cut that out, my mother might see you."

"I'm sorry Asia, I'll go." He slid down into the seat. "By the way, you look great with paint spots on your face like that."

She smiled. "Hey, I'm sorry if I came off a little rough on you but I've got this policy, ya know? But I dig you, we see eye to eye on a lot of things, which is rare. But we can be friends okay?"

"Sure. So how about meeting me for a friendly drink later?"

"Okay. Meet me at the country club at 9:30."

"Fine buddy, see ya then." He drove off smiling widely.

"Who was that?" Rebecca called out, "He looked familiar."

"You remember Timmy, Cymone's old boyfriend?"
"Yes, the one with the pretty eyes."
"Well that was Rae, Timmy's best friend."
"Oh, he's kind of cute, is he single?"
"Mother please. I'm getting in the shower."

Asia looked at the time on her dashboard, it was 9:38. She pulled into the lot of the club. She spotted him immediately. He walked over to her Jeep and opened the door for her.

"I thought you had second thoughts." He nervously rubbed his baldhead.

"I had a tight schedule tonight. But I made it."

He walked to Timmy's car and opened the passenger side. "Come on, let's go."

"Where to?"

"The beach." He said.

He drove to South Beach and parked. He pulled out a bottle of Champagne and a blanket and grabbed her hand. "Let's go buddy." He smiled.

They talked for hours, mostly about past relationships. Asia stood up and walked close to the water. The moon was almost full and bright. The breeze was warm and she wanted him more than any man in the world. He came up behind her; she turned around, grabbed him by the collar and kissed him passionately.

"Friend's huh?" He chuckled and kissed her again.

"Shut up and kiss me." Asia demanded. She was in no joking mood. She wondered why she had crossed the line. Why with him? It didn't matter anymore. She wanted him and that was that. He kissed her hard.

She pulled back from the kiss and looked deep into his eyes. "Let's go." She said.

"What?" He smiled.

"Let's go, and make it fast before I change my mind."

He kissed her again and grabbed her hand and led her back to the car. He drove quickly to Oak Bluffs where he and Timmy were staying.

The minute they hit the bedroom, clothes were flying. Asia could not believe the passion that enveloped her. She had not gone after a man with such ferocity since Greg in the early days. Her kisses were strong and deep. She felt all of the tension and anxiety flow through her body and pass through her lips. When she pulled away from him she had to focus on his face because she was lost in the intensity, his image faded she was thinking of Greg. She pushed him up against the wall and continued.

Rae was in awe. Never had he met a woman so aloof but so hot. He wanted her more than life itself. He knew it was almost a sick obsession with her, but he didn't care. He knew that she wanted him and that was all that mattered. *Asia Blake wants me. If the pussy is as good as I hope I know somebody up there loves me. Oh shit I can't believe it, she's going...ah...down on me and it's the...oh... the best fucking head I've ever had. Oh shit.*

Asia slipped into her ultra sexy voice, "Rae, I have only two questions for you."

He quivered, "Yes?"

"Do you have any condoms?"

"Yes I do, a whole box."

"And....,"She ran her tongue from his navel to each nipple and to his ear, stuck her tongue in it till he purred, and continued, "When was the last time you've been fucked properly?"

Rae melted; he picked her up and carried her to the bed. He mounted her and worked his way down. He was searching for the jewel that her delta possessed. To taste her was all he wanted, her nectar was sweet and intoxicated him, and he knew this was it, she had to become his.

Rae's snoring awakened Asia. She studied him. He was sleeping like a baby. She sat up and looked straight ahead and locked her eyes on her reflection in the mirror. She pulled her knees under her chin and thought about what she had just done. *Wait a minute; I slept with a married man, so what? He's the one who stood up before God and his family and made vows to someone, not me.* She thought back to a conversation she had with Yeva, her producer at the station.

"Asia if you fuck a married man, that doesn't mean some bimbo is gonna come along and fuck your husband."

"Well Yeva, how can you be so sure?"

"Look Asia, the bottom line is if your man is gonna fuck around, then he will. It has no bearing on what you did as a single woman trying to get yours."

Asia still studying herself in the mirror thought, *Yeah, I'm just trying to get mine, that's all.* She nudged Rae to awaken him.

"Yes, Asia what is it?"

"Come on, get up, I want to go home and I need you to take me to get my car."

He tried to kiss her but she could not respond. She was confused and was not sure how to treat the situation. She saw no need to cuddle and enjoy the afterglow that was only for the privileged. Moreover, Asia was not at all comfortable with the idea of getting comfortable with Rae. She knew it was not the nicest way to behave, but fuck it; she was not put here to be nice. Protecting her heart was her number one priority.

The air was cool and the sky was clear. On the ride to the country club parking lot, Asia still had nothing to say.

"You have not said a word. Did I do something wrong."

"No Rae, everything was fine."

"Did I not satisfy you or something?"

"Rae, you were fine, actually pretty good." That was a lie, he was incredible, but she knew she had to play it cool.

Rae pulled the car off the side of the road.

"What's up?" Asia questioned.

"Exactly," Rae was getting upset, "What's up?"

Oh I get it, she thought to herself, *another insecure brother who can't hang when a sister isn't falling at his feet.*

"Rae, I'm tired, it's late, and could you please take me to my car?"

"Why are you doing this? A few hours ago the passion was so intense and strong, but now, you won't even look at me."

"Rae, listen, we can be friends, hell, we can even fuck again, but don't think I'm going to fall in love with you or anything because it cannot and will not happen, okay?"

"So you are saying that falling in love with me is out of the question?"

"I refuse to let it happen."

He smiled and saw it as another challenge; he was beginning to like her twisted games of control, never realizing that it was no game. Asia just wanted to keep a firm hold on her emotions, and masking them was the best way to do that.

He pulled back onto the road and turned into the country club parking lot. "Well Asia, here you are. I just want you to know that I'm feeling certain feelings for you but I'll play this your way."

Asia smiled inside, never once revealing her excitement. "Fine, I'll talk to you later." She pulled herself out of Timmy's car and climbed into her Jeep. She felt strange because she knew Rae was looking at her, that same way he did in the liquor store, as if he were studying her every move. She felt a chill and didn't look back as she drove off.

Rebecca paced and thought of her father. Asia was not home and as usual, insomnia was in full effect.

I have done well, she said to herself. *My kids are almost gone; Josh will probably stay in Malibu once he graduates. Asia is close, but out of the house. William and I are still friends after thirty years of marriage.* She looked up to the sky. *I did it daddy.*

"Mom, what are you still doing up?" Asia hated to do the walk of shame in front of her mother.

"Did you have fun?"

"Yes. And you know I hate it when you answer questions with questions."

"Well, I was just thinking about my Daddy. He loved this house."

"Yes Mom, I know." Asia kissed her mother on the forehead and went to bed.

After a week the house pulled together nicely. The week was over and the house was rented out for the last two weeks of the summer. Asia was excited about getting back to work. She became punchy if she stayed away from work or the computer for too long.

After stocking up the car, Asia took another look around to make sure she had everything.

"Well Ma, I think that's it."

"Okay, let's move out."

The doorbell rang. It was a delivery person from the flower shop.

"Delivery for Asia Blake."

"That's me." Asia signed and gave her a tip. The card said, "I miss you, my radio doesn't sound the same without you. Hurry back. Rae." Beneath a mound of cellophane were a dozen white roses.

"Oh my God, they are beautiful. You have not gotten flowers like that since your fights with Devin."

"Yeah, I know."

"Who are they from?"

"That guy Rae, Timmy's friend."

"Oh, the handsome one, how nice."

"No Ma, It's just okay. Are you ready to go?"

CHAPTER TWO

"It's" the One Thing

YOU GOT A DOZEN MEN BEHIND YOU, YOU GOT THE FELLAS ON THE FLOOR, YOU'RE TOO PRETTY IN THE DAYLIGHT WHICH KEEPS THEM COMING BACK FOR MORE

When Asia got back to the loft, her machine was filled with messages. One from Yeva, three from Sam, two from Cymone and seven from Rae.

The summer had ended abruptly. The winter was rolling in smoothly attempting to steal away those lovely autumn days. Asia was tired and needed something, a break, a vacation anything. It was a cool November Sunday morning. She decided to head to her folk's house early for the ritualistic First Sunday of the Month Dinner.

Asia jammed to Maxi Priest as she drove to her parent's house. Rebecca was trying out a new vegetarian dish while William cried that African- Americans need to become a homogeneous people, and come together to re-elect David Dinkins.

"What we need honey is our own political party, then we could rise above as a people." William wrinkled up his round cocoa colored face.

Asia walked in and kissed her father.

"Asia, you should have moved to New York, instead of Hoboken, and then you could vote for Dinkins." William professed as he munched down on a piece of celery.

"Asia shook her head after kissing her mother. "Daddy, even though you don't live in the city, you could have worked on his campaign or gone out to register New York voters."

"You know I'm too busy for that." William headed back out to the front yard to rake the mounds of leaves. Asia smiled to herself as she thought of her political activist of a father. He was a dedicated follower of anyone giving the white man a hard time. Al Sharpton was his hero. William's motto was 'I'm not anti-white, just pro-black.'

"How's the book coming along?" Rebecca asked.

"So-so. I need a source of inspiration. Maybe a vacation or something." Asia munched on a piece of lettuce.

"A vacation? We were just at the Vineyard a little over two months ago."

"I know, I know but I'm suffering from writers block and I need something to jog me out of it. How long till dinner is ready?"

"About fifteen minutes. While you are waiting, why don't you finally go through your mail cluttering my desk?"

"Good idea."

As Asia walked up the stairs to the study, Rebecca called out "All of your stuff is in the manila folder on the top left hand side."

Asia smiled as she read the letter from her twenty-year old brother Josh. He was a first semester sophomore at Pepperdine. "Hey Ma," Asia called out. "I got a letter from Josh. He's begging for money again."

"Must I remind you that he sent you some of his allowance when you were in school and wrote home for money?" Rebecca called back.

Asia smiled. "Yeah, but he just did that to impress Sam, remember, he thought he was in love with her, and he wrote all those love letters?"

Makin' Happy

"That was some heartache he suffered when she met Wayne."

"Well I guess I could spare a few dollars." Asia flipped through some more mail and found and unusual looking envelope. She quickly opened it. It was an invitation to Greg's wedding. Her face was flush, her heart raced. She read it over again. Her face tightened and her head throbbed.

Asia met Greg when she was in high school, while vacationing on the Vineyard. She hated him instantly. He was arrogant and too smart for his own good. It was as if he was a male version of herself, which turned her on. They fought the moment they met. The thought of him repulsed her until the night they were at a party, he was depressed over a broken romance; Asia was the only one who would listen. She made him laugh. He was the only man that she was physically attracted to and still liked his mind.

Five years after they met, they were doing internships in Boston. Greg opened up to Asia and admitted that he loved her more than just a friend. They spent an entire week in bed before returning to school. The relationship was off and on for years. Their bonding was emotional and explosive. They fought constantly and never agreed on much, but for some odd reason, Asia always believed that he was the man for her.

After finishing medical school, Greg moved to Texas. They tried to make it work but the distance became an issue. The money and time were scarce to invest. Asia refused to leave the station to move to Texas, she loved Greg, but her career was more important. Often she wondered what life would have been if she had moved to Texas with him. She figured she would have never gone back to graduate school, publish her first book, or have the success she has now at the station. Greg had difficulty understanding Asia's refusal to give up everything, pack up, and move to Texas. After all, he thought he was the best thing that would ever happen to her. Being so egomaniacal, he also could relate to Asia's "self first" philosophy.

Asia was pissed. She always hoped that when it came to the game of finding a partner and grinding the others nose in it, she would be victorious. On the other hand, she was somewhat relieved that Greg was going to become a dead issue. *Why can't we be friends?* She asked herself. *Yes, I will bury the hatchet, I will go to this wedding and prove to Greg that I am fine and I can handle this.* She wiped the tear rolling down her face and looked at the invitation again. There was a note saying, "I'll need you there. Love, Greg." Asia felt a chill up her spine and decided that she would call Greg to accept.

Asia wanted to get away; she figured her trip to Texas would do her some good. Sam had wanted to go to Jamaica for Thanksgiving but the station had too many promotional events and Asia had to stick around. Sam and Cymone went without her.

She pulled herself up from bed and drew open the curtains that covered a wall-sized window. She looked out to the New York cityscape and longed for summer. November already, she could not believe it. She wondered if Sam and Cymone were having a good time in Jamaica.

She had just gotten her period and considered it a bright side to not going. *Vacation is a drag when you have your period*, she thought.

She thought of Rae and got a sick feeling in her stomach. They saw each other for a little over a month once she got back from the Vineyard. Asia broke it off when he announced that he wanted her to meet his wife.

"It'll be easier then. She already is a fan of yours, if I introduce you two, she'll trust you. Then we can go out, be seen in public and she won't suspect a thing."

That whole idea was sick to Asia. Since Rae, Asia decided to be alone for a while. Men was something to be sworn off, especially the married ones.

Makin' Happy

She thought of Greg a lot, and couldn't believe that he was going to be married in two weeks. Devin left her mind as quickly as he entered it. She tried to write in her journal but she had nothing to discuss. It was another holiday and she was alone. She was getting used to not having a man around this time of year. At least she had her family. She laughed to herself, *if someone told me ten years ago that this is how my life would be, I'd laugh at him or her, how sad.*

She decided to leaf through past journal entries and she began to notice a pattern in her emotional behavior. When she had her period she was sappy, emotional and felt a need for love in her life. The two weeks after, she was confident, independent and strong. The week before she hated men and the entire patriarchal society. She read some more and was interrupted by a telephone call from Rae.

"I know you don't want to have anything to do with me, but I wanted to wish you a happy Thanksgiving."

"You're right and thanks." She hung up the phone, turned off the ringer and got into the shower.

Asia didn't eat much and she wasn't very social. She made a plate for later, and then headed to the city to do her show.

Lance, Asia's best friend since childhood called her at the station. "I have big news, come over after the show." Was all he said.

"Okay Lance, after the show, I'm there. It'll be around eleven okay?"

"Fine, just get here."

The ride to Lance's house seemed unusually quick. Asia was excited to see him. It had been two months since they have seen each other. They went to school together since Mrs. Greene's second grade class. After graduating from Harvard, he took over his father's investment firm, one of the largest black owned firms in the country. Lance lived on a five-acre ranch in Ramsey, a graduation present from his father. He and Charla, Asia's first cousin, had been living together for about five months. Asia was amazed at how far they had come. Charla was sort of the sister she never had, so they were quite close growing up. Lance had a crush on her since they were kids. Who would have guessed they would be living together, especially since they never really got along? It wasn't until college that Charla would even give him the time of day, and now they were happily living together. Their house was the spot for parties and interesting gatherings. As Asia drove up the winding driveway, she was greeted by Spike, the Old English sheep dog she gave Lance.

"Asia." Lance called out from the front door."

"Hey Lancie," Asia gave him a big hug and kiss. "So, what the fuck is so important that you couldn't tell me over the phone?"

"Well come on in and I'll tell you."

Asia walked in, kicked off her boots, threw her coat over the banister and plopped down on the couch. "Where's Charla?"

"She was here; she left a little while ago. The families did dinner together, she is going to stay at her mom's crib tonight so they can be at Short Hills Mall at the crack of dawn for black Friday, hey you want some turkey, we've got plenty of leftovers?"

"No thanks, I ate at the station, the boss had dinner catered to those of us who were working tonight and I had a plate from moms, I'm kind of sick of turkey at the moment." She got up and headed for the bar, "I will have a drink though. So what's up?"

"This is what's up." He reached into his pocket, pulled out a black velvet box, and handed it to Asia.

Asia's eyes grew wide. "Oh, Lance." She opened the box, revealing a five-carat perfect diamond stone. "This is stunning." Asia felt tears well up in her eyes.

"So, do you think Charla will like it?" He asked nervously. "I've already picked out the setting. It will be done by Christmas."

"Lance, you know she' going to love it. However, you know Charla; she will probably think it's too big. Especially since she's so petite."

"I know, but my mother and I agreed on this stone being a wise investment."

"Don't worry, she'll love it. So Christmas is the time?"

"Yeah, the stone will be placed in the setting the week before and I'm going to ask her to marry me at our New Years Eve Party."

Tears fell down Asia's face.

Lance took the glass out of her hand and sat down next to her. "What's up? You wanna talk about it?"

"That's just it Lance, there is no 'it' to talk about." She wiped the tears away. "You and Charla have 'it', Sam and Wayne have 'it', Ken and Barbie, Dick and Jane have 'it'. I'm twenty-seven years old and I don't even know what 'it' is or who to find 'it' in." She sobbed some more.

Lance cradled her and kissed her on the forehead. He reached into his pocket and pulled out a pen, he placed it in her hand. "Don't look for 'it', for 'it' will find you, until then write."

The flight to Texas seemed to take forever. Asia brought her laptop computer so she could work on her book; she was almost finished but still was suffering from writers block. It had been almost four weeks since she got the invitation and after speaking to Greg, she convinced herself that he really needed her friendship. She had to keep reminding herself that they were friends before they became lovers, and she couldn't give into some whimsical passionate feelings. As the plane pulled up to the gate, she shut her eyes, trying to remember what Greg looked like. It had been almost two years since they've seen each other. All she could remember was the sad look on his face when she turned down his proposal of her moving in with him.

Asia looked for him through the crowd, and then she noticed a driver standing with a sign that read "A. BLAKE".

Asia walked up to the gentleman and said, "That's me Asia Blake."

"Good evening Ms. Blake, I will be taking you to the hotel. Have you any bags checked?"

"Yes."

"Follow me Ms. Blake." He escorted her to a long black limousine waiting outside for her. She handed him her tickets. "Please wait here while I get the rest of your luggage. While you are waiting, have some champagne, I shouldn't be long."

"Asia poured herself a glass of champagne and called Sam to let her know she arrived safely. "Sam, you're not going to believe this shit but he had a limo come get me."

"Wow, I'm impressed."

"I guess he's doing well down here."

"Asia, I don't care what you say; I think he still has the hots for you." Sam cautioned.

"Sam, he's getting married tomorrow, please. Listen could you call my parents and just let them know that I arrived safely?"

"Sure, listen, have fun and be careful."

Asia quickly downed a glass of champagne and poured herself another. She leaned over and turned on the CD player. Maxi Priest was crooning "Wild World." That was her and Greg's song. She sang along. She opened the sunroof and took a deep breath of the warm Texas air. She felt free, relaxed, and excited about seeing Greg.

Greg arranged for Asia to stay at the Hotel Adolphus in downtown Dallas. Asia thought it was odd that he put her up in a hotel separate from the other guests.

Asia felt like a queen with the abundance of southern hospitality. Her suite was equipped with a fresh fruit basket, a dozen roses, and a hot bubble bath had already been drawn for her. Greg's thoughtfulness had not changed. As she took her bath her mind drifted to the night they met at the party, hung out on the beach and talked all night. He was in a drunken stupor, but all he kept saying is that he was going to be such a big success that no woman would ever hurt him again. Asia tried to convince him that no matter how much money and power one has, love and caring is most important. If you treat people properly, they will do the same to you, Asia told him. He thought she was kidding and he laughed and laughed. Then he picked her up, swung her over his broad shoulder, and slammed her into the water.

"Your beauty knows no bounds." He said in a low sexy voice. He sounded mellow like a Miles Davis tune. Asia jumped up and reached for her robe.

"Jesus Greg, you scared me." She slid into the thick white terry robe. She tied the belt and gave him a hug.

"So how was the flight?"

"Great. You almost gave me a heart attack though."

"Sorry. So how are you, how's your mom and dad?"

"I'm fine. They are fine. They just couldn't understand why I came down here to see you marry another woman, my mom called it emotional suicide."

"What do you think about me marrying another woman?" He placed his hands on her waist and attempted to stare into her eyes, but he couldn't pin them down. Asia had the eyes of a butterfly, hard to catch.

Asia, ignoring his stare, walked away from him into the sitting area, searching for the bar. He licked his lips as he watched her sexy wide hips sway in front of him. She smelled delicious. "Well, I've convinced myself to be happy for you." She headed to the bar and poured herself a ginger ale with a slice of lemon. "Besides," she continued, "it's not like we were planning a future together or anything. I mean, I did what I had to do, and so did you. You are a success in your field, and I am in mine, this means that we will be sharing it with other people that's all." She handed him a glass and said, "I'd like to toast to you a long and happy future, and may you always get what you want." *So what if your ass is fine, so what if you look just like Rodney Peete. I am strong. I can deal.* Asia thought to herself.

He put his glass down. "What if I told you that it's you that I want?" He grabbed her by the arm and pulled her closer to him. He pressed his large body against hers. Asia felt him rising against her leg; her heart began to pound. His face was barely an inch away from hers. He parted those beautiful lips, revealing his perfect teeth and smiled. "Look me in the eyes and tell me that my marrying someone else doesn't trouble you."

Asia was royally pissed, but to let him get to her was not in the plan. She grit her teeth and took a deep breath. "Gregory," she said calmly, staring him in the eye, "your marrying someone else does not trouble me." She lied, but she did it so well.

"So that's it?" He was getting angry; he lightly shoved her away from him. "You didn't come here to stop the wedding, or even ask me to consider making love to you one last time."

"Why you selfish, mother fucker, is that what you thought?"

He just looked at her blankly.

"Here I thought that I had such a good friend in you, that maybe we could salvage what was left of our friendship. Now you have the audacity to reduce my visit to one last fuck?"

"But Asia..."

"Don't fucking flatter yourself, yeah you are fine but dumb as hell, now get out."

"I paid for the room, you get out."

"You know what? It doesn't matter, because I'm outta here. I'm going back to Jersey tonight. But I'll tell you one thing the room is in my name and if you don't get the hell out I'm calling the police." She went ballistic. "Now get the fuck out!"

Asia slammed the door behind him. She was too pissed to cry. She plopped down on the bed and made two phone calls. One to the airline to change her ticket and the other to Sam to pick her up at the airport.

Makin' Happy

Sam's townhouse was a wreck. Wayne had been living there for two months and it looked as if a cyclone hit the place. They had just finished making love. When he rolled off her, she took a deep sigh, "Wayne how much longer do you have in school."

"Well if I do summer session, I'll be finished by August of next year."

"Does that mean that you will start cleaning up after yourself around here?"

"Hey, before I moved in you were a slob, don't blame me for all of this."

She wrapped the sheet around herself and made a path through the mound of clothes on the floor and she headed for the bathroom. "That's it, I'm tired of this place looking like shit. And since you started school again I can't deal."

"Sam I know I'm sloppy, but if I'm not trying to make you happy, I'm at class or working. And you know this degree is important so that I can get promoted."

She stood in front of the mirror inspecting her teeth. She was a teeth fanatic. "Hey, didn't you say some of the boys down at the station own a cleaning service?"

"Yeah, Tom and Joey why?"

"Well, I was thinking," she walked back into the bedroom, "it makes no sense for the place to look like this. You're a cop, and I'm an executive, let's put our money together and use Tom and Joey's service." She walked back to the bathroom. "Will you look into it when you go to work tomorrow?"

"Sure boo."

As she reached to turn on the shower, the phone rang.

"Asia, what are you doing calling here now?" Wayne chuckled. "I thought you and Greg would be going at it."

"Oh shut up you fool, give me the phone." Sam snatched the phone and playfully hit Wayne. "Yo Asia, what's up?"

"Sam, I'm coming back to Jersey tonight. I'll explain it all to you later, but could you please be at the airport at 12:45?"

"Sure. Okay let me get a pen. All right shoot...Delta...flight number 113...12:45am got it. I'll see you when you get in."

Wayne kissed Sam's thigh. "What happened?" She sounded really pissed.

"I don't know." Sam reached to hang up the phone. "Hey, let's go to a movie or something; Asia's flight won't be in for another four hours."

"I've got a better idea."

"What's that?"

He ripped of his robe exposing his erectness. "How about letting me wax that ass?"

"I knew there was a reason why I suggested that we live together; you always have such good ideas." Sam reached her hands out and pulled him to the bed by his waist. "And your ass isn't so bad either."

Wayne mounted Sam, looking down at her like a warrior about to attack his prey. He quickly entered her, thrusting his muscular body back and forth. Sam raised one leg and rested it on his shoulder, using her calf to pull his head down forcing their lips to join. "You are the best, absolutely the best." She said with her lips touching his, she forced her tongue into his mouth. "Now fuck the shit out of me."

Sam paced as she waited for Asia to deplane. She looked out the window, and then noticing her reflection, checked her teeth.

"Sam!" Asia yelled, Sam turned around abruptly.

Sam ran up and hugged Asia. "Wanna talk about it?"

"What's there to talk about? Greg is a fucking prick. What else can I say?"

"Are you okay? Did he try to rape you or anything?"

"In a way, not physically, but emotionally. I wouldn't let him though. I just expected things to be different. I suppose I gave him more credit than he deserved."

"Hey, let's get your luggage and swing by Visage for a glass of wine, they're open till three." Sam tried to sound upbeat.

"That's the best offer I've had all day."

Asia and Sam walked into Visage and headed straight for the bar.

"Two White Zinfandel's please." Sam shouted over the music. "Damn it sure has gotten loud here." She said scrunching up her face.

"Maybe we are getting too old for this scene." Asia shouted back.

"So Asia what are you gonna do?" Sam sipped her wine and got serious.

"Do about what?"

"You know, you're twenty-seven years old, and the guys you choose to get involved with are assholes. When are you going to pick a nice one and settle down?"

Asia sipped her wine. "Where in the hell is this shit coming from? Have your parents been calling you a spinster again?"

"No, they called us, me, you, and Cymone spinsters."

"Fuck your parents. Don't start with that shit again. I can't believe you sometimes. Must I live my life and be judged incomplete because I don't have a man?"

"That's not what I'm saying Asia."

Asia squinted her eyes, "Let me tell you something..."

"Excuse me, aren't you Asia Blake?" A young man sitting beside Sam asked.

"Yes, I am." Asia held her finger up to Sam, "hold that thought."

"May I have your autograph?"

Asia smiled and nodded. She signed her name on a cocktail napkin and handed to the young man. "Now where was I? Oh yes, like I was saying I have accomplished more in my unmarried, no-child having twenty-seven years than many have in a lifetime."

"True but I was just..."

"Ah, you were just listening to the bullshit that society sends out."

"Asia I just want to see you happy. There is this new guy on the force and Wayne was telling me that he's single."

"Sam, cut it out. Look, I'm smart, successful, I have wealthy parents, I make a bit of change and to top it off I'm a public figure. I'm a threat to a lot of men. Besides, who needs the hassle of a relationship? I can get dick when I want it and this way I don't have to wake up next to it if I don't want to."

"It's just that you are so beautiful and I don't like to see you alone. And AIDS is out there."

"Sam let's change the subject before you depress yourself and tell Wayne I said thanks but no thanks."

They both began to laugh. "You know Sam; I'm not bothered by the fact that I don't have a man. I'm just upset because I lost a friend today."

"Or you mean found out that you never really had one in him. Will you ever forgive him?"

"No, I don't think I ever will."

"Do you miss him?"

"Sort of. I miss what he used to be. The Greg I saw today I didn't know. I guess I'm just sad because I thought I had found 'it' in him."

"Found what in him?"

"Oh nothing." Asia thought of that night at Lance's house and smiled. "By the way Sam, did I mention that I finished my book?"

CHAPTER THREE

Original Sin

DREAM ON WHITE BOY, DREAM ON BLACK GIRL AND WAKE UP TO A BRAND NEW DAY, TO FIND YOUR DREAMS HAVE WASHED AWAY

Asia woke up squinting. She fell asleep with the curtains open and the sun was shining brightly considering it was December. She buried her face in the mound of pillows on her bed. The phone rang. She jumped up and looked at the clock. It was twelve thirty. She answered on the third ring.

"Yes." She tried to sound awake.

"What are you doing there?"

"Lance, I live here."

"You know what I mean. Last time I saw you, I was dropping you off to catch a flight to Texas. What did that bastard do?" Lance didn't care much for Greg.

"Let it suffice to say that he pissed me off and I came back home last night. Sam picked me up."

"Are you okay?"

"Yes baby, I'm fine. So if you knew I wasn't going to be here, why were you calling?"

"Well, the party is upon us and I wanted to know if you would contact that balloon place and have them come do the decorating."

"Sure. So are you nervous?"

"Not until I picked up the ring after having it set."

"Don't worry, everything will run smoothly."

"I hope so. Oh I forgot to tell you, Jay Feiner is coming down for the party."

"The Jay Feiner? Your roommate from Harvard? Wow I have not heard that name in a long time."

"He'll actually be in town on the twenty-sixth and he'll be staying on through the New Year."

"God I had such a mad crush on him, for a white guy he was pretty hot."

"Well perhaps you can tell him that, we are all doing dinner the night he comes to town."

"Are you finally giving me your blessing to date a white man, especially Jay?"

"You know how I feel about sisters dating white boys but Jay is different. Besides, when we were all in school, I knew Jay and you would never work out. You all the way in Atlanta, him in Cambridge, what a mess that would have been. But now, hey who knows?"

"So I take it he's still single, you know how important that is."

"Yes, he's single and actually requested your company when I told him that you were around and available."

"Lance thanks for being my boy. Kiss, Kiss."

"Yeah, yeah. Just please remember to call that balloon place and put the twenty-sixth on your calendar.

"Gotcha, now get off my phone I'm going back to bed."

Christmas day came and went. Asia pretty much lost the spirit. Nevertheless, the snowfall was light and pretty, so that made the holiday bearable. She was looking forward to dinner with Jay, Lance and Charla. Lance had called and said that they would meet her at the station at ten once she wrapped up her show; they would all dine in the city.

Makin' Happy

Asia secured the headphones on her head, turned up the mic, and gave the station call letters. "And that was a classic from the royal king of reggae Mr. Bob Marley, going out to Marlesha in Queens. Well this ends my session, This is Asia Blake saying bye-bye, coming up we have Subtle Sounds with Vernon Hayes so don't touch that dial."

As Asia stood up, she looked at her reflection in the glass from the control room. When she looked beyond it, she noticed Jay looking into her eyes smiling.

She exited the studio to find him; *the* Jay Feiner standing there with his arms open wide.

"Jay," she ran over to him and hugged him. "What has it been five years? How are you?"

"I'm great. Look at you. You look terrific." He smiled nervously. "We listened to you on our way here, and in the lobby. You sound great on the air." As he spoke, the words were quickly lost with Asia. She was so caught up in his dreamy chestnut eyes; she was amazed at how good he looked. "You still have those dimples." He reached out and touched her cheek.

She blushed. "You look great yourself. Old age agrees with you."

He chuckled. "Are you finished?"

"Yes, I've just gotta go get my bag and stuff. Where are Lance and Charla?"

"They're down in the car."

Asia scurried around collecting her coat and bag. She dipped into the ladies room to freshen up. She felt like she was in high school, excitedly touching up her lipstick.

The rest of the week Jay and Asia were inseparable. At the party, once the announcement was made and Lance presented Charla with the ring, Asia and Jay spent the evening talking in the den. Away from the crowd, they sat in front of the fireplace, playing Scrabble, laughing and holding hands.

"Asia I've had such a good time this week, thank you." Jay leaned over and kissed her gently on the lips. "I'd like to spend more time with you if that's possible."

"Jay, I'd like that. How do you feel about this Boston, New Jersey thing?"

"Well, I'm in New York a lot on business and, I hope that you would come up on the weekends."

Asia was thrilled. This, she thought, would be the perfect situation; he's close enough without being up underneath her all of the time. She was excited that Jay was interested. She felt that because of her size, five feet, ten inches size sixteen dress, that most white men were not attracted to her. But Jay being six feet five inches put her at ease, she liked big men.

The countdown began.

Ten, Nine, Eight...

Jay stood up and reached out for Asia's hand.

Seven, Six, Five...

She reached up, took his hand and stood up.

Four, Three, Two, One...Happy New Year!

"Happy New Year Asia." He leaned over and stroked her face.

"Happy New Year Jay." She kissed him.

Asia woke up and stumbled to the bathroom, wiping the sleep out of her eyes she attempted to view herself in the mirror. "Lovely darling!" She looked horrible. Her eyes were puffy, her hair pointing in every direction. She wasn't sure what to make of her situation with Jay. As she put coffee on and headed to the stereo, she couldn't decide what CD to play...Micky Howard, "ah it's sort of a blues Sunday," she thought out loud.

Makin' Happy

Jay popped into her mind again. *Why can't I stop thinking about him? Because I want to think about him, that's why.* The internal conversation ceased. The phone rang, Asia answered hoping that it was Jay; he was supposed to call the night before. It was Samantha.

"Asia, it's me, did I wake you?"

"No, I was just making some coffee. Hey when did you get back in town?" Sam had been to New Orleans attempting to close a deal she had been working on for months.

"I got back late Friday Wayne and I went to the city yesterday, so I'm just getting home."

"How's it going with him in school?"

"I miss him a lot but it's for the best. I'm glad he's decided to go back to school and finish his BA, besides, since he did the winter session, he'll be finished in May instead of August."

"Cool, so did you close the deal?"

"Yes and this could mean a big promotion for me, I meet with my boss tomorrow. So what are your plans for the day?"

Asia sipped on her coffee. "I'm doing dinner with my parents and Josh tonight. Hey you should come; Josh still has that crush on you ya know."

"That might work, depending upon my unpacking and doing my laundry. Hey girl, are you down for JE's for breakfast?"

"Hum, I am kind of hungry and I could go for their catfish and grits."

"Great then meet me there in an hour"

Asia rushed around the loft, hoping that she could shower, dress and make it to Newark in an hour. While scrubbing her back, she thought of Jay again. She knew that Sam would ask many questions since they haven't spoken in a while. "Why a white guy?" She'll say. "We all knew that your bourgeois self would eventually jump the fence." She'll continue.

Drying herself off Asia was prepared, though she knew deep down that she expected a relationship with someone white to be

...different... better, that was the myth she had been buying into. Was it better so far? Not really, it feels the same. Once the initial romance was over, Jay was just another guy, calling at a different time than the time he said he would call. Sometimes late for dinner dates. She concentrated on the little things he would do because she was afraid of being taken advantage of. She knew Jay was a good guy, but he was still a man and the natural distrust of someone white loomed over her head. She wanted to let go and just love him, just relinquish control. But how could she? She had never given a man that much power since Greg and that was almost ten years ago. Should she empower a white man? A person, who by virtue of the color of his skin, and his gender, the world was an open oyster. She knew that she respected him and he respected her, to Asia that was key. The only struggle within was recognizing that Jay was not exactly the image of her dream man. She thought about the possibility of something long term, could she hang? Could she deal with those snickers she hears when they show affection publicly? Could she handle raising a child of mixed heritage? However, the one thing Asia loved was "those looks" from brothers, as if she has betrayed them in some way. "Fuck them, if they had it together in the first place I wouldn't be with Jay now." She blurted out. *How in the world am I going to tell my father?* She thought to herself. Ah it's not that serious, or is it?

She wiped the steam off of the mirror and looked at herself, "Oh my God, I'm standing here thinking kids and long term, could I be in love with this man?

JE's was packed as usual. The crowd was an interesting assortment. There was the after church crowd, the important political figures dressed down, and the array of couples who had been fucking all night long heading in for a good home-cooked meal.

The ambiance was nothing special, very 70's, but the food was scrumptious. Asia believed that it was the best soul-food restaurant in the state, possibly the tri-state area.

When Asia arrived Sam was sipping a Piña Colada. JE's also made the best mixed drinks. Asia stopped to speak to some friends at a nearby table, licking her lips just thinking about the Piña Colada waiting at the table for her.

"I decided to order one for you; I figure I'd drink it for you if ya didn't get here before I finished mine." Sam continued, "I also ordered catfish and grits for you."

"Thanks." Asia sipped her drink.

"So, are you gonna make me ask about *him* or what?"

"I'd prefer the 'or what' actually." Asia sipped her drink again.

"So what's up with Jay?"

"Well, things are cool, he's a nice guy and we have fun together."

"Cymone told me that you guys have been like peas in a pod, and at Lance's party you two were inseparable." Samantha stated as a matter of fact.

"Well I suppose we have been, when he's here, but Boston is starting to appear further away. So I'm trying to take this one day at a time, ya know, trying not to think about him, I can't get all hyped and shit."

"Oh well that's cool."

'Cool!' That's all you can say? Asia thought to herself, where's the interrogation? Where are the wise cracks? Can't you see I'm lying through my fucking face? Can't you see that I'm in love? That all I do is think of him, and I can't talk to Lance when I get mad at him, because of their friendship? What happened to the good old days when you used to beat me up till I told you the truth? Damn sister girl you sure are getting old, taking my bullshit at face value. Asia was amazed

at Sam's acceptance. Sam was talking about a Jazz club in New Orleans, totally unaware of Asia's frustration and bewilderment.

"Sam, I'm not being totally honest with you..."

"So what else is new?"

"What do you mean by that?"

"Asia, I've known you for a long time now, when you are ready to tell me the truth, I'm here, so what's the real deal?"

"Well, I think I'm in love with him."

"I can't say that I'm surprised, I mean you fall in love quickly and often."

"Yes I know but I really think I'm in love."

"Is it for the right reasons?"

"What in the hell is that supposed to mean?" Asia began to jump on the defensive.

"Asia are you sure you love his mind, his spirit, his soul? Or is it what he represents? Think about it."

Before Asia opened her mouth to rebut, she thought about it. What scared her is that she really wasn't sure. She took a bite of her catfish and looked at her reflection in the window. "It's cloudy today isn't it?"

◆

As she drove home jamming to Queen Latifah, Sam wondered if she went a little rough on Asia. *No I wasn't rough on her. Asia is a thinker and I like to throw something profound her way every now and then, besides it helps me feel like I can hang with her. She gets into these intellectual artist modes and I enjoy making her think. I always know that I have her when she changes the subject to something off like the weather.*

Sam stepped over her luggage and headed for the phone, she wanted to tell Cymone about New Orleans and breakfast with Asia.

Makin' Happy

"Hello." Cymone answered as she exhaled a cigarette.

"Hey it's Sam, what's up?"

"Yo, what up, how was the trip?"

"It was nice, I finished up down there, and I have a feeling I'm going to get promoted for this one."

"That's great...Brianna can't you see that mommy is on the phone? Sorry Sam my brat is messing with me, anyway, did you get some quality time in with Wayne this weekend?"

"Yeah, we met in the city yesterday. I had brunch with Asia today."

"Damn, you all didn't even invite me."

"Sorry, it was just a last minute thing, trust me, nothing formal."

"So where did ya'll go?"

"JE's. Check this out; she thinks she's in love with the Bostonian."

"Well I can't say that I'm surprised. Is she happy? Brianna stop pulling that...no...If you touch it I'm going to...damn it, look what you did! Listen Sam; let me call you back, this girl just knocked over my basket full of sewing notions."

Sam hung up and chuckled. She wondered what it would be like to have a kid. She was feeling the urge. *Well*, she said to herself, *Wayne will be finished with school soon, I think it's time we talk commitment and future, after all, I'm not getting any younger.* She pulled herself up from the bed and headed to the living room to unpack. She stopped at the mirror and turned sideways, holding her stomach, trying to imagine how her size twelve body would look pregnant. She giggled and ran out of the room.

Asia opened the door to the empty loft, trying to forget her discussion with Sam. What does Jay represent? She asked herself. Asia knew exactly what Sam was talking about.

Asia reflected on a conversation a few weeks ago with Sam, Charla and Cymone. It was a bit of a black man bashing session...

"Well hey; I'm tired of black men and their inability to accept responsibility for themselves and their actions." Asia declared.

"Sorry, but nobody can love me like a brother can." Sam chimed in. "Asia you are just like a white girl yourself, I can't believe that it's taken you this long to go out and get a white guy."

"Yea Asia," added Cymone. "Wasn't one of your line names 'White Girl' when you were pledging?" She began to laugh.

"Yes, but hey, that has nothing to do with anything. Just because I am articulate should not make me any less black, besides look how dark my skin is and I've never wanted to be white or lighter. You have nerve to talk Cymone, you're light bright and damn near white, trying to pass for a Puerto Rican, running around in loud ass colors, and teaching Brianna how to speak what little Spanish you know."

"She's got a point there." Sam said nodding at Charla. They all cracked up.

"But it shouldn't matter what color you are." Charla said.

"Yes Charla you are right, unfortunately, in America it matters." Asia continued. "Okay, until Jay, I've never dated a white guy, I've had crushes but that's it, but I swear brothers piss me off when they run around here with these white girls on their arms, especially the successful, hard working brothers."

"Tell me about it." Sam cut in; "they walk around oblivious to the fact that it is like a slap in the face to sisters everywhere. Whenever I see a brother, I just wonder how his mother feels about that white bitch on his arm, and then I wonder if her family even knows about him."

"People should be colorblind when it comes to skin color." Charla declared.

"But Charla," Asia rebutted, "you are a black woman, we all are black women, and we should be seen as that. I'm sorry but when white people grin at me and start talking that 'I don't see color' bullshit, I leave them alone because the bottom line is if you don't see color then you don't see me."

"True," Cymone jumped in, "but let's face it, da brotha's are fuckin' up, in a big way. So what are we single sisters supposed to do, especially those of us with kids?"

"Well, I guess that could work for you with the men who like kids." Charla answered. "Or it could work against you with men who don't like kids. But you're lucky because Brianna is a great kid."

"Getting back to that interracial stuff," Sam added, "I think black people date white people because it represents a voice saying 'look society, I overcame, I got the forbidden fruit on my arm.'"

"What about whites dating blacks? Charla queried.

"It's kind of the same thing, but white girls are just looking for a big dick. I think white men live in the fantasy of a master/slave relationship when they go for black women." Sam answered.

"Well I don't know about all that but I do know this..." Asia paused and bowed her head and raised her hands, "sistah's, if we want companionship on our intellectual, and economic level, we are going to have to leave our race...that is the bottom line."

"Well look at me." Charla said quietly, "I've got Lance, he's hardworking, he's educated, and he's black."

"And he's rare." Cymone interrupted.

"That he is." Sam added. "Look at me and Wayne; we both come from hard working middle-class families."

"Yeah but you've got an MBA, he's just now finishing under grad, and he's a cop, you are an executive with a Fortune 500 company." Asia stated.

"Don't forget to mention that she makes more money than him and probably will continue to if he is serious about being a career officer." Cymone said. "Now don't even look this way, because you know my taste in men leaves a lot to be desired. I like them young and dumb, so I can call all the shots."

"What about you Asia?" Sam asked, "Devin wasn't so bad."

"Yes he was." Asia cleared her throat. "Well even though he was only raised by his mom who didn't have much money, he did have some class, but he lacked motivation, remember, he dropped out of school and I don't think he's gone back. In addition, he was a weirdo who had serious problems with the fact that I came from a family with some money and that my father spoiled me. Every time we got into a fight, he turned it into an argument about how bougie I was. He was just insecure and jealous."

"I liked him." Charla smirked, "Then again, I like everybody."

"Charla, you are my girl and all but damn you can be so naive. I'm just glad that you and Lance are getting married, and then I don't have to worry about you." Asia grabbed her left hand and held it up singling out the five-carat diamond on her finger, "you my dear are very lucky. So are you really ready to make that move?"

Charla started beaming, "Yes I am, October can't come soon enough. Now let's talk Bridesmaid gowns."

The telephone rang and brought Asia out of deep thought.
"Hello."
"Asia, it's Jay, how ya doing?"
Asia took a deep breath, attempting to not sound excited, "Hi darling' how you doin'?"
"I'm okay, but I'm missing you very much."
"Jay, I miss you too. How's everything up that way?"
"Well I can't complain. Listen Asia, what are you doing this coming weekend?"
"The girls and I might hit the mall, we've all got some shopping to do and you know everyone is having a springtime sale, why do you ask?"
"Well, I... um, my parents are flying up from Miami and I, ah, I want you to meet them."

Asia gasped a rush of joy and horror came over her. She went into the bathroom and closed the door. "Jay, are you sure about this, I mean we've only been dating for a few months, and…"

"You just don't get it do you?" He sounded frustrated, "don't you realize that I care for you? I want this to develop into something more than just weekend visits."

She pulled the toilet seat cover down and sat on it. "Jay, I don't know what to say. I…, um, I…"

"What, New York's most talkative disc jockey is at a loss for words? What is the problem? What are you so afraid of?"

"Jay, I really care about you, you know that, but I'm afraid of being hurt."

"Asia, I care so much about you, and to stand here and say that I will never hurt you would be a false promise, and you know how I feel about promises being feeble attempts to predict the future. But I can tell you this, I will do what I can to make you happy, I'm tired of being out there. I'm tired of not being certain how you feel. I want to do whatever it takes to ease your fear of being hurt, but I cannot do it alone. Are you with me on this?"

"Jay," Asia had a tear rolling down her face, she tried to keep her voice from trembling, "I'm with you, but can I ask you something?"

"Sure, what's up?"

"Do they, your parents, do they know that I'm black?"

"Yes Asia, they know."

She sighed. "What time should I be there?"

CHAPTER FOUR

Don't Change

RESOLUTION OF HAPPINESS, THINGS HAVE BEEN DARK FOR TOO LONG, DON'T CHANGE FOR YOU, DON'T CHANGE A THING FOR ME

Driving to Morristown was going to be a pleasant experience since the new highway was opened, and the temperature had warmed up to almost seventy-five degrees. Asia put the top down and picked up Sam.

"Well Sam, I'm kind of glad you are coming with me tonight. I think I'm going to break the news to my parents."

"Girl your daddy is going to hit the roof, man, I couldn't have asked for a better time to visit the Blake residence." Sam chuckled.

"Not only daddy do I have to worry about, but Josh will probably not be too happy, he always liked Devin."

"Girl, I don't think it will have anything to do with Devin, I bet he will be pissed to know that his big sis is running around with a white guy. Remember, by the time he was nine, you had him reciting the phrase, 'Don't bring her home if she can't use our comb'."

"Yeah, but it's different, I have a difficult time finding a black man on my economic and intellectual level, that's not married or gay. You see, a brother can never say that he can't find a quality sister, economically and intellectually balanced to suit him, not only that but we black women come in such an array of colors, sizes and shapes, why would they ever look elsewhere? The pickings are much better for them. If Josh ever came home and said that he can't find a sister as a partner, I'd be able to find one for him."

"I agree with you to a certain extent but you know how black men get, you just need to be prepared."

"Sam, I suppose your right. But hey, it's not like Jay and I are getting married, we are just becoming a couple."

"A couple of what is all I ask." Sam laughed alone at her own joke.

Dinner went smoothly, Rebecca made Gazpacho with homemade bread, fruited chicken salad, and William made ambrosia for dessert. Josh followed Sam around and hung on her every word.

"So guys, I'm going to Boston next weekend." Asia announced.

Sam's eyes grew wide.

"Oh really," William, continued, "Is this business or pleasure?"

"Well daddy, it's sort of pleasurable business."

"Asia, you have the life, so what could possibly be so pleasurable about business?" Josh frowned and took in a spoonful of ambrosia.

"Well, do you guys remember Jay, Lance's roommate from college?" Asia assumed this would be the safest way to approach it.

"Vaguely." Rebecca sighed as she tried to remember.

"Well he has invited me to come up and hang out for the weekend, we've been hanging out for a few months and his folks are coming up from Miami and...."

"Hey, isn't he a white guy?" Josh interrupted.

"Yes he is white." Asia stared blankly at Josh.

"His parents? What is going on here? Hanging out?" William was confused. "Why are you going to meet some white boy's parents?"

Sam smirked; she knew the performance was about to begin.

"Daddy, first of all he's a man, not a boy. Secondly, we have been seeing each other and I think he's kind of cool. If you have an issue with the color of this man's skin, I'd just as soon not discuss this any further with you."

"Well if dad doesn't take issue with it, than I am. What's going on sis?"

"Josh, we have just been dating." Asia attempted to remain calm. "If it bothers you, then you will have to deal with that yourself."

"Oh, I get it." Josh got sarcastic, "I don't ever recall hearing 'don't bring him home if he can't use our comb' I only recall 'her' in that sentence."

Rebecca jumped in, "Josh that's enough. William, leave her alone. Asia is almost thirty years old; she can do what she wants. If the man is treating her well then I don't give a damn what color he is. Now let's change the subject." She turned to Asia, "how's your book coming along dear?"

"All I got to say is your mom is mad cool, she was like Superwoman saving your ass." Sam chuckled as she shared her observation with Asia.

"Tell me about it. It's always been us against them in my house. Men will gang up on ya and hang you out to dry if you give 'em half a chance." Asia looked straight ahead as she drove up the highway.

"Yo, let's stop by and see if Cymone is home, maybe we can go grab a drink or something."

Asia and Sam went straight to Cymone's house. She was as usual on the telephone and yelling at Brianna.
"So where are you tramps on your way to?"
"To Visage to have a drink." Sam answered.
"Do you think you can get a sitter for Brianna? After all, you say we never invite you to go anywhere." Asia added.

Cymone convinced her mother to watch Brianna for a few hours. She pulled on a pair of jeans and a cable knit sweater. She had long straight hair; she whisked it up into a ponytail and put on a dab of lipstick. "All right, I'm ready to go."
The three of them sat at the bar at Visage. Cymone puffed away on her cigarettes.
"Hey Cymone, have you heard from Timmy lately." Asia asked.
"Yeah, I saw him a couple of weeks ago. He took me out for dinner and a movie."
"So," Sam chimed in with her favorite question "did you get some?"
"Yes and it was slamming, thank you very much." Cymone exhaled her cigarette. "Oh my God, speak of the devil." She pointed to the front door. Timmy had walked in, with Rae.
"Ladies, to what do I owe the honor?" Timmy exclaimed as he made the rounds, kissing Sam, then Asia and lastly Cymone. "You all know Rae Underhill."
Rae's eyes met with Asia's. Asia was suddenly feeling uncomfortable. It was strange confronting someone she was mean to on the telephone.
"Hi Asia." He rubbed his head and whispered in her ear, "Do you think I can speak to you privately for a minute?"
Asia smiled an awkward smile. "Sure."

She followed him to the restaurant side, to the booth in the back. He turned around and pointed, "Have a seat right here; I'll be right back, White Zinfandel right?"

"Yes." Asia watched him walk away and was amazed at how good he looked. She had to remind herself that he was a strange one.

He walked back to the booth carrying their drinks. He placed hers down first, and then his, then he sat down. "So, will you at least speak to me now, and listen to what I have to say?"

"Rae, about the..."

"No." He interrupted her. "I have the floor now. You have been really fucked up through this whole situation and I wanted to let you know that."

Asia was shocked. No one calmly sat and spoke their mind so well since Greg in college. She looked directly into his eyes and leaned forward. "First of all, maybe I was but, why are you bothering me with this shit now?"

"Asia, believe it or not, I thought we were friends. Then you just started bugging. Not taking my calls, hanging up while I was in mid-sentence, and that hurt."

Asia again was caught off guard. She was surprised by his honesty. She thought to herself of all of the times someone had pissed her off and she never confronted him or her. She found herself admiring what Rae was doing. "Rae, you are right, I guess that I should have just told you what the problem was instead of hanging up on you all of the time. So how are you doing?"

"I'm fine. I've missed you a great deal and I'm going through a pretty nasty divorce."

"Oh Rae, I'm sorry to hear that. But you know it's for the best right?"

"Absolutely. I just wish it could be all over with. The holidays were somewhat tough, especially since you wouldn't speak to me. But enough about me how are you?"

"Well I just finished my second book. It should be in print by the summer. Things are well at the station and I'm in love."

"That's great. Who's the lucky guy?"

"He's an old friend from Boston. Yes things are going well for me."

"So, since you are in love, I suppose us getting together would be out of the question."

"Rae, as long as we remain friendly. I would not be opposed to spending some time with you."

"Great. What are you doing tonight?"

"Well, I was having drinks with my friends and I'm about to go join them. Why don't you give me a call later and maybe we can have dinner this week."

Asia pulled herself up from the booth and led herself back to the bar where Cymone and Sam were sitting.

"So what did he want? Is he planning for you and his wife to go shopping together?" Sam snickered. Cymone laughed.

"No. Actually, he's getting a divorce. He just wanted to clear the air between us."

"So is it clean?" Cymone asked.

"Yeah, it's all right." Asia sipped her wine and smiled.

Asia stepped off the plane squinting her eyes as she looked for Jay. She felt a tug in her stomach when she realized that he wasn't at the gate waiting for her. She decided to walk toward the terminal, hoping to run into him. As she approached the escalator, Jay came around the bend.

"I am so sorry. Traffic was an absolute mess." He rushed at her and kissed her on the lips.

Asia kissed him back and smiled. "It's okay."

"Did you check any luggage?" He reached for her overstuffed Gucci travel bag. "Let me take that for you."

"Nah, I hate to check luggage. Besides I'm only here for the weekend."

He smiled impishly. "I was hoping I could convince you to stay longer, like maybe forever."

Asia felt strange. Moreover, Jay's comment did not make her feel any better. *What the fuck is that supposed to mean?* She asked herself. *Why can't I find someone who would be willing to move for me rather than them trying to uproot me?*

"My parents are so excited to meet you, especially my mom." Jay picked up a playful tone, trying to forget Asia's strange behavior.

"Great, I can't wait to meet her either. How's your dad feeling?"

"He's okay; he just can't stand the cool weather."

"Could you blame him? Besides Miami is so fun and warm. Boston is so gray and cold." Asia continued. "Can I tell you that in all of the years I've visited Boston, the sun has only shined twice?"

"So does that mean I can't get you to move up this way?"

Asia stopped walking. "Jay, what is going on?"

"What do you mean?" He asked innocently.

"I've been off the plane all of fifteen minutes and you have already made two references to me living here. What is up?"

"Asia, it's no secret that I love you. When I love something I want to keep it close."

"And when I love someone I let them be." Asia resented being referred to as a thing. She continued walking, and then she realized that she was walking alone. She turned around and looked at Jay. His eyes were fastened upon her in shock. She walked up to him, wrapped her arms around him, and laid on the charm.

She whispered in his ear. "So, what time do we hook up with your folks?" She stuck her tongue in his ear and sucked his ear lobe.

"Seven-thirty." He whispered, his voice was trembling. There was something about her touch that could instantly loosen him up.

"Great let's go back to your place so I can freshen up okay?" She kissed him on the cheek.

When they arrived to Jay's car in the garage, he had a dozen red roses sitting on the passenger seat waiting for her. She hated red roses.

Asia was nervous and uneasy about meeting the Feiner's. She felt comforted by the fact that Mrs. Feiner was looking forward to meeting her. She wrote poetry and when Jay told her about Asia's book she went out and bought a copy. She read it from cover to cover, hoping to learn something about the author and black life. Gloria Feiner was still trapped in a sixty's time warp. She looked like a gray haired flower child. She waited in the lobby of the Westin Hotel for Jay and Asia to arrive. She wore her hair wild and out, it framed her face as if she was an angel. Her clothing was loose and baggy but elegant and tasteful. It was obvious she enjoyed spending her husband's money.

As Asia and Jay entered the hotel, Gloria calmly walked over to them. She was a tall beautiful woman with chiseled features. She kissed Jay and held her arms open to hug Asia. Asia leaned forward and was relieved that the hug was sincere.

"So this is Asia. Finally we meet." She spoke softly and she was very articulate.

"How do you do Mrs. Feiner?" Asia smiled as she spoke.

"Please, call me Gloria."

"Mother, where is Pop?" Jay asked anxiously.

"I told him I'd phone the room when you arrived."

"You and Asia have a seat, I'll get him."

Asia couldn't believe Jay left her alone with his mother. She seemed friendly so Asia decided to jump into conversation.

"So, how was the flight from Miami?"

Makin' Happy

"It was just dreadful. I hate to fly. I don't really drink but I must when I fly so I can fall asleep."

Asia chuckled. "Yes I understand how that can be."

"So Asia, I must tell you that I enjoyed your book. You are quite a talented young woman."

"You read my book?" Asia was in shock.

"Yes. I write a bit myself so when Jay told me you were a published author, I had to run out and get a copy."

"Well Mrs. Feiner...excuse me, Gloria, I am very flattered. So what kind of writing do you do?"

"I dabble in poetry."

"Oh, I would love to read some of it sometime. I started out writing poetry myself."

"Really? I would love to share it with you. Tell me, do you play squash?"

"No, just racquetball and tennis, that's it for me."

"Good. I hate to exercise. Jay and his father are going to the club for a game of squash tomorrow morning. What do you say if we get together, do brunch, read a little poetry and shop?"

"Gloria that sounds like a fantastic idea." They both giggled.

"All right ladies break it up." Mr. Feiner playfully growled. He took Asia's hand in a very familiar way and shook it as she stood up. "You must be Asia." He chewed down on his unlit Cuban cigar. "Nice to meet ya."

"Mr. Feiner, it's a pleasure." Asia smiled nervously. She felt like she was speaking to a gray haired, tan, older Jay. He and Jay looked exactly alike. He had a sharp, subtle wealthy look about him. He was an attorney in Miami, often representing undesirable types involved in drug and other smuggling scandals.

"The pleasure is all mine dear." He smiled and kissed Asia on the cheek.

"Okay, let's get a move on before we lose our reservation." Jay announced.

Dinner went smoothly, much to Asia's surprise. She had heard horror stories from friends about white people not embracing blacks when involved with their children. On the ride back to Jay's apartment, Asia thought about the tension that would flow if she brought Jay to meet her family. *Talk about a switch, I guess it's a myth about blacks being so embracing; Dad and Josh would have a fit.*

"So what are you thinking about?" Jay interrupted.

"Oh just about how nice your parents are, now I know why you turned out so well adjusted."

"What do you mean?"

"Well, ya know, you are a pretty together guy, now I know why, that's all."

"Well I must admit, my parents are very cool, what about your parents?"

"Well, they're okay, especially my mom. She and I are very close. We are like sisters, we talk a lot, and we travel together. It's kind of nice to know that I have her, I'd be lost without her."

"What's her name?"

"Rebecca. And my dad's name is William."

"So when will I get to meet Rebecca and William?" Jay smiled.

Asia felt a twist in her stomach. "Soon."

CHAPTER FIVE

New Sensation

LIVE BABY LIVE, NOW THAT THE DAY IS OVER, I GOT A NEW SENSATION, IN PERFECT MOMENTS, IMPOSSIBLE TO REFUSE

On the flight back to Jersey Asia went right to sleep. She had difficulty sleeping in Jay's bed for some reason; maybe it was because she knew she didn't belong there. She loved Jay, but she realized that she wasn't in love with him. As the plane landed and shuttled to the gate, she looked out the tiny window and watched the rain pour onto the ramp workers.

She smiled to herself when she thought about Gloria. Her poetry wasn't the best but it was nice to see her attempt and share, Asia was touched. *Too bad I have to end it with Jay, why can't I just exist without pressure from a man to do something he wants me to do?* She asked herself. *What am I going to do with him? How do you tell someone that you don't think its right between the two of you? Boy this is weird, I have had to dump many of men but never have I had to let someone so nice and sincere go, but I can't string him along.*

As she walked off the plane, she hoped that Cymone would be on time picking her up from the airport.

"Brianna, sit down while I'm driving, and put that seat belt back on." Cymone raced up the highway trying to get to Newark Airport before Asia had a fit about her being late again.

Cymone was always late. When she dies she plans to arrange it so that her corpse arrives late to her own funeral, it would be her way of getting the last laugh. She owned countless watches and clocks set ahead of normal time and she was still always late. Internally she knew it was her only way to be rebellious. She was running extra late because she had spent the weekend with Timmy and had to pick Brianna up from her mother's house before getting Asia.

"Mommy, where is Auntie Asia?"

"She's at the airport honey, we are almost there."

"Good 'cause I miss her."

"I bet she misses you too pumpkin, in fact, let's ask Auntie Asia if you can spend a weekend with her real soon." Cymone smiled to herself.

"Yeah mommy, I'd like that."

"Okay Bri, look out the window for Auntie Asia while I drive. When you see her, yell."

Brianna spotted Asia immediately and let out a piercing scream of joy. "Mommy, mommy, there she is I see Auntie Asia."

Cymone pulled over abruptly in front of Asia, popped the trunk and got out of the car.

"What fucking time is it Cymone?" Asia said under her breath so Brianna wouldn't hear her.

"I'm sorry yo, but I was at Tim's and then I had to race back to East Orange to my mom's crib to get Bri. So what's up? How was Beantown?"

"Well it was good but I've decided that I'm not in love with Jay anymore."

"This is so typical of you Asia; you do that shit all the time."

"Oh mommy said a bad word." Brianna yelled from the backseat.

Makin' Happy

"Yes mommy is a bad girl." Asia said laughing. She turned to Cymone "What do you mean by that?"

"Well," Cymone lit a cigarette and adjusted her rearview mirror and sped off. "You fall in love quickly then as soon as they do one thing you don't like, you're outta there kicking up dust in their faces."

"So what? I'm supposed to be in situations that make me happy, if I'm not happy or feeling the way I used to, why should I stick around?"

"Because it's called compromise, putting your time in, ya know?"

"No I don't know. Are you saying that I should stick with somebody, even if I feel nothing for them, hoping that the feeling will come or come back?"

"Basically." Cymone looked straight ahead.

"Cymone, maybe that's the way you want to live but it's not for me. I'd just as soon spend the rest of my life alone than fake the funk."

Brianna started laughing, "Auntie Asia, what does 'fake the funk' mean?"

"Well it means to pretend. To make believe you want to do something when you really don't want to. To be untrue to yourself." Asia shot a glance at Cymone. She said nothing.

Asia quietly thought to herself. She wondered why everyone had bought into the philosophy of being unhappy to achieve happiness. *What is happiness anyway?* Asia looked over at Cymone as she drove and sang Naughty by Nature's Hip-Hop Hooray along with Brianna. *And what the fuck does she mean putting in your time? Is this love or a jail sentence? Maybe I just wasn't cut out for a relationship anyway, too much work, too much of a hassle. All I want is to pack up my Jeep, buy a little place on a beach, maybe Miami or Malibu and me and my Old English Sheep Dog will ride off into the sunset and live uncomplicated lives near the ocean. Who needs a man in the picture? As long as I have batteries, I'll be fine.*

"So Asia, Bri and I have to run to Short Hills, you wanna come to the mall with us?"

"Yes Auntie Asia, come shopping with us."

"To spend time with you Bri, anything, how about your mommy buying us root beer floats when we get there?"

"Yeah Mommy root beer floats." Brianna cheered from the backseat.

When Asia got back to the loft, there was a message from Jay. He said that he knew something was wrong and he wasn't going to force the issue. He had decided to leave the situation alone and he'd be ready to talk when she called. Asia breathed a sigh of relief. She figured she'd call him later in the week and discuss it then. She was bursting with ideas and energy to start her new book. It was to be about a black female detective who falls in love with a bad seed cop and she has to bring him down.

As she was typing away on the computer the phone rang.

"Asia it's Rae, can you talk?"

"Rae, its okay I was just doing some writing, what's up?"

"Well I was thinking about you and what you said."

"And what was that?"

"That we could be friends. Is that okay because right now I could really use a friend."

"Well I was away all weekend, my place is a mess but if you want to come over, feel free."

"Great. I'll be there in about an hour, can I bring you anything?"

"Surprise me. I'll see ya in bit."

Rae paced the floor as he spoke to Asia. He was pleased when she invited him over. He liked Asia, admired her in fact and that scared him. He had never fucked a woman he admired. He went into the bathroom and splashed on some After-Shave. *Surprise me?* He thought to himself, *what in the hell does that mean? She* likes White Zinfandel, so that and a loaf of French bread should do the trick.

He threw on a sweater and his raincoat and headed for Jersey.

When he arrived to Asia's loft his heart rate sped up. *Why am I nervous? What have I got to be nervous about?* A lot actually. Rae had an idea for a television series and he wanted Asia to help him write the pilot episode. He was afraid that she would shoot him down. There is nothing worse than being rejected by someone you look up to.

Asia answered the door wearing flannel boxing shorts and a T-shirt. Her hair was blow dried straight and curled on the ends it flowed down her back and framed her face. She looked like a princess. Her nails and toes were done, for Rae that meant a lot. She was not only smart but also beautiful. *How can I get you to be mine?* He thought to himself, *there's gotta be a way.*

Asia escorted him in, thanked him for the wine and took his coat. She was again surprised at how good he looked. He was the only man she met who smelt good all of the time and looked better each time she saw him.

"So what are you working on?"

"Just kicking around this idea for my next book, I've got a meeting with my publisher next week and I cannot show up empty handed." She poured them each a glass of wine. "So what's up with you?"

"Well, I have this great idea for a screenplay well; it's actually for a TV program, perhaps a mini-series, to spin off into a weekly show."

"Rae, that's fantastic."

"Well I'm glad you think so, because I want you to help me with it. You see I'm good at coming up with ideas but you are so descriptive and I think your wit and humor is just what it needs.

Asia was getting excited. She never thought much about writing for television. She was willing to give it a try. Besides, she genuinely liked Rae, especially after they cleared the air.

"I'm in."

Rae smiled. His heartbeat grew steady when he heard those magical words. *She's in.* He thought to himself. *I've got Asia working with me, this is good, but I can't blow it. I've gotta come to her with my shit correct, cause I know she's a force to be reckoned with.*

"Rae, I said I was in. What's wrong?"

"Oh nothing, I just get lost in my thoughts sometimes. So I can count on you to help me out?"

"Yes, what were you thinking about anyway?"

"Oh, nothing."

"Only men."

"What do you mean by that?"

"Well, men seem to be the only people who can get lost in their thoughts then when I ask about them, they say they were thinking about nothing."

"I know women who do it too."

"Yeah, I'm sure you do but the difference is, we really do think and just choose not to share. I believe that men actually get caught up in thinking about nothing."

"Asia," Rae got serious, "if we are going to work together, may I suggest something?"

"Sure, what?"

"Stop being so damn cynical about men."

"Gee Rae, that sounds more like a demand than a suggestion, you aren't trying to tell me what to do are you Rae?"

"Oh, I wouldn't dream of telling you what to do Asia, not in a million years."

"Smart man." Asia took a sip of wine. "You see, I called you smart, how about that?"

"Ah, she's coming around." He chuckled.

"You know Rae, I think us working together might be a good idea, perhaps you can help me change the way I see men."

"Right now I want to change the way you see me."
"Now my dear, you have got your work cut out for you."

Asia and Rae sat at the computer and put together a story outline. It was almost three in the morning and Asia was getting a little punchy. She was also a little tipsy, as she typed away some more; she glanced over and noticed that Rae had fallen asleep on the sofa. She studied him. She liked to watch people as they slept. She felt it was a way to observe people with their guard down. There was something so raw and sensuous about the way he breathed, it fascinated and excited her. For some reason she was feeling drawn to him.

It's his mind, she thought, *he really knows how to use it*. She got up and fetched a comforter from the hallway closet and threw it over him. He snuggled to it as if he were a child with a security blanket. "Looks like you're in for the night buddy." She whispered. She shut off the computer and the lights, locked the door and headed to bed.

"Asia?" She heard Rae call out.

"Yes?" She whispered.

He whispered, "I'm sorry I fell asleep on ya. Do you mind me crashing here tonight?"

"It's okay." She whispered.

"Asia?" He whispered back to her.

She again whispered, "Yes Rae, what is it?"

"Can I ask you something?"

"What?" Still whispering but she was getting aggravated, he was starting to remind her of Josh as a little boy the night before Christmas, all excited that he couldn't sleep, so he'd pester her.

"Why are we whispering?" He whispered and began to laugh.

Her voice returned to its normal tone. "Rae shut up and go to sleep."

"Asia?"

"What?"

"Can I sleep with you, I mean beside you."
"No."
"Can't blame a guy for asking. Oh well good night, or shall I say morning, because technically it's..."
"Rae," Asia interrupted, "shut up and go to bed."

Asia diligently wrote for the next two months. She was coming along well on her book and Rae was making the right contacts for them to sell their idea. Since that first night Rae had stopped making advances at her. Their relationship was strictly professional but that made Asia want him more. Summertime was approaching and Asia was feeling restless. She needed to get away and it was time to get up to the Vineyard and prepare the house for the summer rentals. She decided to invite Sam and Wayne, Cymone and Timmy, Charla and Lance and Rae. After calling all the girls to make the arrangements, she thought about how to invite Rae. It was purely a couple's thing and even though nothing was going on between them, he was the closest thing she had to a date. He had become her close pal and confidant. *Besides, now that things are taking off for us professionally and I've gotten to know him as a friend, a true friend, I'd like to spend some quality cool out time with him.*

Rae was on his way over, there was an opening at a gallery in Newark and Asia asked Rae to join her. Asia paced nervously; she began to talk to herself aloud. "I cannot believe that you of all people are nervous over Rae, of all people. This is ridiculous, just come out and ask him, point blank. He's your buddy, he'll love the idea."

The doorbell rang. She stopped dead in her tracks and ran her fingers through her hair. "Well champ here it goes." She said to herself as she opened the door.

"Who are you talking to?" He asked as he walked in.
"Myself."
"Well are you ready?"
"Not just yet, let's sit for a minute."

"Uh oh, what did I do? You've got that 'Rae, you fucked up' look in your eyes."

"Rae, I'm surprised at you, I thought you knew me better than that. I just have to ask you something, that's all."

"Good. So, what's up?"

"Well, I was just talking to the girls; ya know Cymone, Sam and Charla."

"That could be dangerous."

"Yeah it could be."

"What is the fearless foursome cooking up now?"

"Well, we were talking about heading up to the Vineyard week after next. With the wedding coming up, none of us can really afford to go away-away."

"That sounds nice. Since we've been working on this project, I know you haven't really gotten a chance to hang with the girls."

"Yeah, that's true. But there's more."

"Okay, what else?"

"Well, Charla is bringing Lance, Sam is bringing Wayne and Cymone and Timmy are going to hook up."

Rae nodded his head, feeling sort of left out. "That's nice." He cleared his throat and nervously asked, "May I get personal?"

"Sure."

"Who are you going with?"

"Well I was kind of thinking that you've been working really hard and could probably use a break so I was wondering if you'd.... ya know?"

Rae was thrilled, he was leaping inside but he maintained his composure. This was the moment he was waiting for. *I knew it!* He thought, *I knew that she'd eventually come around hot damn it!* He said nothing.

"Well?" Asia asked impatiently.

"Well what?"

"Don't play games with me Rae, do you or don't you?"

"Do I or don't I what?"

"Rae why are you being so difficult?"

"What...me...difficult? Never. Why don't you just come out and ask me instead of expecting me to finish your sentences?"

"Well you do it all the time. That's what I love about you. You sometimes know what I'm gonna say before I say it."

"That's what you love about me?"

Asia looked around nervously like a little girl who had let the cat out of the bag. She twisted her mouth and whispered, "Yeah, there are certain things I love about you."

"How about me?" Rae looked serious. He took her hands, "do you love me?"

Asia looked at him. She knew she loved him but she wasn't ready to give him the satisfaction of knowing right then. "Rae, why must you always answer a question with a question?"

"It's a habit a picked up from you my dear."

"Touché. So will you be my date for our couples extravaganza to the Vineyard?"

"Do you love me?"

"Will you join me?"

"Yes."

"Good."

CHAPTER SIX

The Swing

It's the swing like a pendulum; it marks the moments as the years go by in an innocent phase, the swing into never-never land

Back on the ferry, this time, she was one of those couples she used to hate. She and Rae held each other as they watched the sunset. For once, all of the pieces seemed to fit. She had finally found a friend, a lover, and a partner. All she ever wanted was to be happy and now she was happy. But how long will it last? She had decided to not trouble herself with those negatives. It was going well and that's all that really mattered.

The wind blew gently; there was still a chill in the air. Rae held her from behind and whispered in her ear, "You know what's so special about us?"

"No, what?"

"We fit. I hold you in my arms and I feel like a hand in a glove, we belong together."

"I'm afraid so. How does that make you feel?"

"Like I'm in heaven."

"Rae I want to read you something okay?"

"Sure what is it?"

"It's a poem I wrote for you. I wrote it last night as I watched you sleep."

"Okay, let's hear it."

"Well it's called Life's Little Rewards." She brushed her hair out of her face and cleared her throat.

Lust lingers
love settles
loving you is one of
life's little rewards.

Conversation enlightens
the bond of friendship tightens
in you I have found
my ideal.

Our souls were destined
to meet, to cross, to merge.
Being with you
has become a constant urge.

I long to tell you,
lick, taste, smell you.
I want to dive into you
and never rise.

The passion is stronger,
I'm wanting you with me
longer, I know...I know...
I shouldn't.

I'm way past my limit,
your loving? I'm knee deep in it
it's just one of
life's little rewards.

She looked up at Rae to find his eyes fastened on her. He shook his head and smiled. He pulled her closer and hugged her tightly, he was completely speechless. They kissed deeply. When she pulled away from him a tear rolled from his eye. She gently kissed it.

"Asia, you have shown me a kind of love like I've never known before."

"What do you mean?"

"I mean, your way of loving me is on a level I've never reached. It's passionate, not silly and playful like others in the past."

Asia was still a bit confused. "You mean no one has ever written poetry for you before?"

"No. Never. Damn Asia, you're so deep, so cerebral. That's what I love about you and your honesty too."

"What else do you love about me?"

"I love the way you look at me, it makes me feel desired and welcome. I love the way you freely express yourself to me. I love the way you say my name, when you say it, it's like I'm hearing it for the first time. And the fact that you are so beautiful doesn't hurt."

"That's kind of nice to know." Asia looked out to sea when she heard the familiar clanking of the buoys. She took in a deep breath and exhaled. Finally, her ship had come in. She no longer felt like she was walking blindfolded through an unfamiliar house. She knew her way around and for the first time in her life, she felt good about her sense of direction.

"Hey what's on your mind?" Rae asked.

"Oh, I'm just getting lost in my thoughts."

"What are you thinking about?"

"Oh, nothing."

He smiled at her. "That sounds familiar."

"Okay you love birds, let's head down to the car, we're almost at Woods Hole." Charla called out.

"Well darling it looks like our vacation is about to officially begin, can you hang?"

Rae put on his best Jamaican accent, "chile, please...I was born hanging."

Asia looked around to see if anyone was looking and grabbed his crotch, "yeah, I bet you were baby, I bet you were."

The crew had decided to go their separate ways for the rest of the evening and agreed to come together for brunch the following day. Sam and Wayne headed for Circuit Ave for dinner. Timmy and Cymone showered, changed, and headed for Timmy's favorite bar. Charla and Lance unpacked the groceries and headed to the beach for an evening picnic. Asia and Rae went straight to bed and made love until dawn.

Sam woke up with the sun beaming in her eyes. She tossed and turned before finally getting out of bed. She yawned as she headed to the bathroom. She looked up when she heard the clicking of computer keys. "Rae what are you doing up?"

Rae was diligently working on the lap top computer. "And good morning to you too."

She yawned again, "Fuck it, I'm on vacation, and I don't have to be cordial."

Rae smiled. "I'm working on an idea for a screenplay, I want to surprise Asia with the story outline and see what she thinks."

"You two have become quite a productive team, I'm impressed."

"Really?"

"Yeah, really. You seem to be one of the few men she likes. I don't know how you did it, but whatever it is you're doing, keep it up."

"Sam, how long have you known Asia?"

"Over ten years. We met our first year in college."

"Has she changed much?"

"Well Asia was pretty sharp then, I'd say she's much more focused now. But she's come into her own I must say."

"Yeah? That's kind of cool. How did you two meet?"

"Well, we met through a mutual friend at Morehouse. He liked pulling people from Jersey together. Anyway, we're at one of his frat parties and she walked in as if she owned the fucking place. I was like get a load of this bourgeoisie babe from the suburbs."

"So she had that attitude back then?"

"Yeah, it was worse then because she was so shy. It was her defense mechanism to act extremely comfortable and confident in uncomfortable situations. Anyway, I didn't like her very much and can I tell you, we didn't speak to each other till spring semester and we were reintroduced at a sorority rush tea."

"Then what, you guy's clicked?"

"Hell no. I hated her even more. But once I found out we were both chosen to be on line together, I figured I'd get to know her during the summer." Sam paused and looked up to the ceiling. "That summer I decided to call a truce and invited her to a party I had. Man, we did shots of tequila all night and got sick together. We bonded. And ever since then she's been my ace."

"And what about Cymone, how does she fit into the picture?"

"Well Cymone and I knew each other from high school. She went to school in Jersey and pledged the same time we did. She met Asia that same night at my party."

"Good morning people, how ya doin'?" Charla shuffled into the living room and planted herself on the couch. "So, what are you guys talking about?"

"I'm telling Rae about the first time I met your stuck up cousin." Sam began to laugh.

"Alright tramp, watch yourself." Asia playfully growled as she staggered into the living room. She plopped down on the couch next to Rae and leaned against him. "What are ya working on?" She asked.

"It's a surprise." He smiled, turned off the computer and planted a kiss on her cheek. Sam stood up and headed for the bathroom.

"So, where are we doing brunch today?" Charla cheerfully asked.

Asia yawned, "It doesn't matter to me, as long as I get something to eat. I'm starving."

Rae chimed in, "Me too." He looked at Asia lovingly.

"Hey Asia," Charla got excited, "remember that place in Edgartown we used to go to when we were kids?"

"Oh yeah, they serve big breakfasts and there's have a great view of the water, Charla that's a great idea."

Sam came out of the bathroom and was greeted by Cymone, as evil in the morning as she wanted to be. "Morning Cymone." Sam giggled as Cymone growled at her.

Sam waltzed into the living room announcing "Evilena has awakened." They all laughed.

"So Rae, how does it feel to be a part of the girls club?" Charla queried.

"I must say, I'm a lucky man." He looked at Sam, then Charla, at Asia, and then he looked up at Cymone who was still sporting a frown and messy hair. "Yes indeed, to be surrounded by such visions of loveliness makes me a very lucky man."

Cymone flipped him the bird and headed back to her bedroom.

The sun was strong but there was still a chill in the air. One by one they filed in and out of their respective bathrooms to shower and shave. Timmy was the last to rise and after a while Asia gave Cymone directions and told her to meet them there.

Timmy bounced out of the shower to find Cymone angrily pacing the floor. "Come on you slow ass, I'm hungry."

"Where is everybody?"

"They got tired of waiting for you."

"Damn, can't fuck with a bunch of hungry black folks can you?" Timmy cheerfully concluded. "Hey baby, come give me some sugar." Timmy headed toward Cymone with his lips puckered. She playfully ran away from him. They chased each other around the sofa. Cymone pulled off his towel and began to snap it at his bare ass, a skill she developed while working as a lifeguard in high school.

"Damn boo, that shit hurts."

"Then move your butt, I'm hungry!"

Cymone and Timmy walked into the restaurant hand in hand, dressed like twins, they both sported white linen shorts and green T-shirts. Cymone had her hair pulled back in her usual ponytail, sporting little make up. Timmy wore a huge smile; his eyes were big, brown, round and clear. His eyelashes were long and curly; any woman would kill for those lashes.

"Morning guys." Charla sang.

"Hey you guys look so damn cute." Lance cracked.

Timmy smiled and shook his head, "Why you gotta go there man?" He reached out and shook Lance's, Wayne's and Rae's hand.

Breakfast went fast and they silently ate. After the table was cleared, Charla jumped in with her cheerleader attitude. "Well now that we've eaten, what do we do now?"

"Well Asia and I were thinking about riding around, maybe drive up to Gay Head and look at some houses." Rae announced, "Feel free to join us."

"I kind of want to go to the inkwell and get some sun, see who's here, ya know." Sam stated. "If you guys wouldn't mind dropping us off, we'd be straight."

Asia sipped her coffee. "No problem."

"Well Asia, how about us riding together? Charla and I would like to drive around and look at some real estate, we're thinking about investing soon."

"Oh, must be nice. Good idea, this way Sam, you and Wayne can take my Jeep." Asia looked over at Timmy and Cymone, "so what are you guys going to do, do you want to join us?"

"Well we wanted to do the Circuit Ave. thing and maybe take in a game of tennis at the club later," Timmy looked over at Rae, "Yo man, you down for a little competition?"

"Hey man, I'm down. Asia can you hang?"

"Hell yeah, Cymone you better practice while we're gone." Asia smiled and winked at Cymone.

"Damn, I haven't played in a long time, but I'll be ready for ya!"

"Alright then." Asia stood up and looked at Lance, Charla and Rae. "Well let's be out."

The days and nights went fast. Asia couldn't believe how well she and Rae had been getting along. Sam and Wayne kept to themselves a lot, just hanging on the beach and shopping, and Timmy and Cymone slept all day and partied all night. If her students could see her, they'd die; Cymone was an undercover party animal. The minute she got away from school and Brianna, there was no stopping her. Lance and Charla lived like an old married couple; their days were detailed and planned. Even when on vacation, Lance was an agenda freak. By the middle of the week they were spending a good portion of their days with a real estate agent.

Asia stood on the roof of her garage, which her uncle had turned into a sun deck. She reflected on the week and looked up to the sky. "Well God, you know I have not been the greatest person in the world, but I try. Anyway, I just want to thank you for blessing me with what I have; strong, healthy family, good friends, and a buddy who I love dearly. Thanks."

Rae stepped out onto the roof with her. "Who are you talking to?"

"An old friend." She smiled. "So tonight we cook dinner as a group, any suggestions?"

Rae clapped his hands and rubbed them together. "Well I was thinking about making my specialty, sea food quiche."

"Yummy. I was thinking about making ambrosia for dessert, but I need to go the grocery store. Wanna take a walk with me?"

"Sure, but let's go back to bed for a minute."

Asia smiled, "Just a minute?"

Rae kissed her. "Longer if you'd wish."

"I wish, I wish."

Asia reached down as he kissed her deeply and stroked his hardness. Her excitement intensified. Rae already had her bra undone and a nipple in his mouth. They maneuvered their way across the deck and through the door. They stumbled into the bedroom and clothes went flying. Asia stopped him in mid kiss, and pushed him away from her. He was surprised. Then she grabbed him by the waist and yanked him closer.

"Get over here you sexy motherfucker," she growled.

His eyes grew wide and his dick immediately sprang up towards her.

She undid his pants and pushed him on the bed. She hungrily took his throbbing dick into her mouth and sucked it like the answers to life's questions would be revealed in his climax. She moaned and slobbered all over him, hungrily sucking him. He exploded into her mouth, feeding her every drop.

He was in love.

Sam and Wayne were busying themselves around the kitchen when Asia and Rae returned from the grocery store. Asia leaned over Wayne's shoulder, "What are you guy's cooking for the big feast?"

"Bar B Qued Chicken Wings and Ribs." Wayne grinned, "My Mother's secret recipe."

"Oh yummy." Asia sighed.

Timmy and Cymone came busting into the kitchen. "Back da fuck up fella's!" Timmy announced as they rushed in with a bushel of steamers.

"Damn y'all are no joke." Sam declared.

"I'm saying." Wayne agreed as he and Rae shook hands.

"Has anybody seen Charla and Lance?" Sam asked.

"Well they were responsible for the wine beer and a desert dishes," Asia continued, "maybe they're at the store rounding up the goods."

"All I know is that there's gonna be some good eating going on tonight." Rae said as he rubbed his belly.

"This is so special," Asia continued, "now a scene like this I'd like to see in a film, positive young brothers and sisters coming together to share in the responsibility of cooking a meal."

"Breaking bread and..." Sam added as she pulled a bottle of White Zinfandel out of the refrigerator, "sipping wine, hey Asia could you pass me a cork screw?"

Asia jumped up, "Sure."

"For real tho', you never see anything like this in a film," Cymone observed aloud. "I'm so tired of all the ghetto films."

"Tell me about it," Sam sipped her wine and continued, "If I see another Boyz N the Hood-type film I'm going to be sick."

"Seriously," Asia got philosophical, "why must all of the problems of black folk be solved in the street? My Dad never solved his problems in the street, neither did his Daddy."

"And why must they all be about men?" Rae questioned.

Asia looked over at him and smiled. He was definitely a man after her heart.

Charla merrily walked into the kitchen with a grocery bag. "What are you guy's talking about?"

Timmy broke it down for her; "we were talking about the lack of positive and realistic images of people of color in film."

"Oh, that's nice." Lance beeped the horn and Charla jumped. "I almost forgot that he was out there," Charla looked over at the guys, "Lance needs help bringing in all the beer and stuff, could you help him out? I hurt my back on the tennis court the other day."

The men filed out of the kitchen.

Charla watched them all exit then turned around to face the girls. "Good, I'm glad they're gone, we've gotta talk."

Asia walked over to Charla; she had never seen her so shaken up before. "Charla what's the deal."

Charla looked around to make sure that they were alone. "I think I'm pregnant."

"Oh shit." Sam blurted.

Asia hugged her, "Are you sure?"

Charla nodded, "yeah, I think so."

Cymone took a swig of wine, "so what's the problem?"

"What's the problem?" Charla whispered angrily, "the problem is that my wedding is four fucking months away, that's the goddamn problem Cymone."

"Calm down Charla." Asia reached for her glass of wine and took a sip. "First of all, you don't know if you are pregnant for sure. Second of all, calm the hell down, getting all upset like this is not healthy for you if you are pregnant."

"Damn," Sam whispered to Cymone, "I didn't know she had it in her to be such a spitfire, still waters sure run deep."

"I'm sorry you guys," Charla started sobbing, "especially you Cymone, I didn't mean to bite your head off; it's just that I wanted my wedding to be perfect."

"Charla, you can still have a wonderful wedding and be pregnant."

"Asia's right honey." Sam added.

"Look at Aunt Sandra, she didn't show till her seventh month. She was pregnant when she got married and no one knew." Asia hugged her as she spoke to her.

Charla wiped the tears from her eyes. "Yeah, that's right, and we're about the same size."

"That's right, so don't worry." Asia kissed her on the forehead.

Cymone and Sam walked towards them and joined in the hug. "Don't worry Charla," Cymone advised, "if you are pregnant the most important thing is that you keep calm and be healthy. Fuck what people think. You and Lance love each other and you are engaged."

"True and you guys would make great parents and that's all that really matters." Sam kissed her on the cheek.

Charla started sobbing and crying hard. "I'm so lucky to have you guys."

"What in the hell is going on in here?" Lance asked with the fellas standing behind him.

Charla walked over to Lance and hugged him and grabbed his hand. "Sweetie we need to talk, let's go to our room."

Lance turned around and blankly said, "call us when dinner is ready, it sounds serious."

Rae looked at Asia and mouthed, "What's up?" and shrugged his shoulders. Asia shook her head as if to say, 'I'll tell you later'.

Everyone was silent as Charla and Lance exited the room. The men were feeling as if they invaded a ladies only discussion.

Cymone looked around and felt uneasy with the silence. "Hey Tim, could you pass me a beer please?"

"Sure." Tim walked over to the refrigerator, "okay, who else wants one?"

Everybody called out "Me."

"Well, let's get this party started." Asia called out as she ran to the stereo in the family room. "Any requests?"

"Yeah I've got one." Rae responded as he followed her. "Would you kindly tell me what the hell that was all about?"

"Charla just had a panic attack. All this looking around at houses freaked her out a bit." Asia kissed Rae and changed the subject, "so what do you want to hear?"

Rae reached for the Disco Classics collection of CD's and loaded them into the stereo. "Let's kill some of this tension with some good, old stuff." Foxy's *Get Off* blared from the stereo.

Makin' Happy

Cymone and Timmy came dancing into the family room. Sam and Wayne followed. "Hey Cymone and Asia, remember this?" Sam started dancing, bouncing her body and head from side to side.

"Aw sookie sookie," Cymone hollered out.

"The Patty Duke, I remember that." Asia said as she followed Sam's lead.

Rae looked around at Sam, Wayne, Timmy and Cymone. Then he watched Asia as she flung her hips and hair. She looked like a black flower child, her skin was deep reddish brown and her hair had flecks of red from being in the sun. He loved her simplicity and naturalness. He watched Sam as she danced methodically and coolly. Her skin was dark and smooth like a Hershey bar, her hair very short, jet-black and slicked back. She was mellow and always composed. Wayne was tall and built like a Lumber Jack, he was coffee colored with short hair, and his muscles flexed with every dance step, and Rae chuckled as he watched Wayne watch himself in the mirror. Cymone was drunk and giddy. She struggled to keep the beat and she grew frustrated as her hair kept flying into her mouth. Her skin was a light golden brown, kissed by the sun. Timmy was thin and short, his body was a darker golden brown and his muscles were forming, his hair was curly on top and faded at the sides, he just stood in place shaking his head from side to side.

When the song ended, Asia asked, "Who's up for a Scrabble match?"

"Not me, but I'll watch." Cymone responded.

"I'm in." Timmy called out, but I'll be right back. He ran out the front door to his car.

"We've got to finish the ribs and chicken, so don't count us in." Sam said as she and Wayne danced to the kitchen."

"I'm in." Rae called out, "come on Cymone, you and Timmy against me and Asia, okay?"

"Alright, alright, let me go get another beer."

Timmy came back in and looked around, "Yo where is everybody?"

"Sam and Wayne are cooking, Asia went to get the Scrabble board and Cymone went to get a beer." Rae looked confused; he knew Timmy was up to something. "Why man, what's up?"

"Yo, I ran into Mark on Circuit and he hooked me up." Timmy pulled out a small plastic bag with weed in it.

"Damn man, I haven't gotten blunted in a long time." Rae's eyes got wide.

"Do you think Asia would mind?" Timmy asked.

"Well we never spoke on it much, but she told me that she used to smoke weed when she was in college."

"Who used to smoke weed in college?" Asia asked as she walked into the family room with the Scrabble game in hand.

"Asia, do you feel like getting blunted?" Timmy blurted out.

Asia hesitated, "Yeah, but not here."

Rae looked at her in surprise.

"Cool, let's go to the beach then." Timmy announced.

"Well, I know Sam doesn't smoke and Wayne is a cop, so he can't." Asia turned around and faced the kitchen, "hey Cymone, grab some beers and let's go for a little walk."

"What?" Cymone peeked out the kitchen door.

"Grab a six and let's go, tell Sam and Wayne we'll be back in a few."

Timmy headed for the car, and then Asia called out, "let's not be stupid Tim, if we're going to get fucked up, we'll walk."

Asia led them to a wooded Area near the compound. She and Rae sat on a log and Timmy and Cymone sat on a huge rock. Asia watched Timmy as he emptied a Phillies Blunt and proceeded to use it as rolling paper.

"Whatever happened to joints?" She asked.

"Girl, joints are out, blunts are in." Cymone continued, "My kids tell me it burns slower than rolling paper and you can fit more weed in."

"Damn!" Asia was in shock, "your kids talk to you about this stuff?"

"Hell yeah." Cymone took a swig of beer, "they know more than us chile."

"Cymone, what grade do you teach?" Rae asked as he pulled on the blunt.

"Eleventh grade English."

"Damn baby and they talk to you about getting blunted?" Timmy asked.

"Sure," she lit a cigarette to kill the smell of weed. She hated the smell. "They need someone to listen to them. Once a week after school, I advise a rap session and we talk freely about anything."

"Anything?" Asia smiled. "Cymone that is great, so that's how you keep up with what's hip and what's not."

"Yes girl. They really are good kids, it's just that living in East Orange, and they are forced to grow up fast. It's kind of fucked up because they are robbed of their childhood."

Timmy took a hit off the blunt, "yeah, they do have it rough, shit I grew up in Newark and we had it rough too."

"Yo man, you know it's different now." Rae looked up at the sky through the trees then took a sip of beer. "That generation has it really rough; we had it easy compared to them. But you went to prep school, that's a different world compared to public."

"Hey," Asia stood up and wiped off her butt, "I've got the munchies, Sam and Wayne should be finished with those ribs."

"I'm with you baby," Rae said as he helped her wipe off her butt.

She playfully slapped his hand. She looked over at Timmy and Cymone, "You guys coming?"

They looked at each other and smiled, "Nah, we're going to chill for a moment." Timmy smiled as he spoke.

Rae rubbed his stomach, "Yo man, don't take too long 'cause you know I can put a hurting on some food."

"Asia," Cymone slurred her words, "Don't let him eat everything, save me some."

"I can't make any promises." Asia smiled and took Rae's hand and led him through the woods.

Charla rolled over to find Lance looking out the window. He was watching some kids from the compound play street football. *I'm going to be a father*, he thought to himself, *damn, I'm scared, and I hope it's a boy. Yeah, I can be the coach of his little league football team. What if it's a girl? Then I'll be the coach of her football team.* He smiled to himself.

"Honey, are you okay?" Charla asked as she rubbed her eyes.

Lance walked toward her and lay beside her. "I'm fine, a little scared but I'm okay. How about you, can I get you something?"

Charla leaned over and kissed him on the nose, "No." she said quietly.

"So, do you want to go ahead and do it now?"

Charla smiled. "Nope, October is the date we set and that's when we're getting married. Fuck what people say or think."

"You've been around Asia too long you know." He smiled. "Are you hungry?"

"Yes a bit." Charla yawned. There was a quiet knock at the door.

Lance opened it, Asia stepped in, closed the door behind her and hugged Lance. "I'm gonna start calling you daddy, so you'll be used to it by the time Lance or Charla Junior comes along."

Lance pulled away and looked at Asia's eyes, "are you okay?" *Damn forgot the Visine.*

"Yeah, allergies. So are you guy's hungry because we have a feast out there."

Lance and Charla followed Asia into the dining room. Sam and Wayne had finished setting up the table. Lance couldn't believe his eyes. "I've died and gone to heaven. Let's eat"

They ate like it was their last meal. Asia figured she'd get up early in the morning, run to the beach and swim off the meal.

Cymone decided to just fast for the next week and smoke a pack of cigarettes a day. Sam didn't care. Charla ate more than most of the guys. Rae figured he'd work out with Asia. Timmy and Lance were both so thin they needed more meals like that one. Wayne decided that he'd do three hundred push-ups before he went to bed.

The weather had taken a turn for the worse. The temperature dropped to the low sixties. Asia built a fire and they all wound up in front of the fireplace. Rae and Asia embraced each other on the sofa. Lance stretched out along the adjacent sofa and placed his head in Charla's lap. Sam and Wayne cuddled on the floor to one side of the fireplace; Timmy and Cymone cuddled on the other.

"This feels good to me." Charla blurted out. She ran her fingers through Lance's hair as she spoke. "Friendship is so important..." she looked lovingly down at Lance, "love is also important."

Asia snuggled tighter to Rae. Sam and Wayne looked at each other and smiled. Timmy looked down at Cymone who was fast asleep. He leaned over and gently kissed her on her forehead.

"True Charla, it is important to have love and friendship." Asia cleared her throat. "I wonder if there are people out there who could be perfectly happy without love and friendship."

Lance lifted his head as he spoke, "sure there are people who can live without it, but define 'perfectly happy'."

Asia opened her mouth but she stopped herself, she wasn't sure how to respond. She thought about her fantasy of packing up her Jeep and moving to a little place on the beach with a dog as her companion. *Could I really live like that?* She asked herself. *I mean, I've always wanted to live an uncomplicated life solo, but would I really be happy? And what the fuck does happy mean anyway?*

"Excuse me for a second." Asia jumped up and ran to her bedroom to find a dictionary. She was determined to actually look up the word happy.

"Where are you going?" Sam asked.

Asia came running out of the bedroom waving her tattered and torn American Heritage Dictionary she bought her first year in college. "Lance," Asia plopped down on the sofa, flipping her hair over her shoulder, "what does 'happy' mean?"

Lance glanced up to the ceiling and looked over at Asia, "happiness is I'm about to marry the woman of my dreams, and we are about to start a family." He puckered up his lips and pulled himself up to kiss Charla on the chin. She nodded her head.

"Sam, Wayne, what about you guys?" Asia asked.

"Finding a housekeeper that won't quit." Sam responded. Wayne shook his head in agreement.

"Timmy, what about you?" Asia brushed her hair behind her other ear.

"Blunts, sex, and money...now that's happiness." Timmy smiled and closed his eyes.

Asia turned to Rae and raised her eyebrows, "and you?"

Rae just smiled and said "you."

Asia grew frustrated, "don't you all see, I asked Lance to define happy, not give me a personal statement on what will make him happy."

Sam wrinkled up her face. "Asia, what in the hell are you talking about?"

"Okay, hear me out." Asia reached over to the coffee table and took a swig of beer. "When I was twenty-one, I thought nothing would make me happier than publishing my first book. Now six years later, I have set different standards for happiness."

"Yeah and?" Sam was still confused.

"So does this mean that happiness is ultimately never achieved? Because once I've obtained what I thought would make me happy, I've set my sights for happiness on something else."

Timmy stood up and stretched, "alright Asia, no more Indonesia for you, how about a cup of tea to pull you together."

"Timmy, I'm fine, I just want you guys to think for a moment, that's all." Asia started flipping through the pages of her dictionary. "Here it is ...happy...characterized by good fortune...

having, showing or marked by pleasure...appropriate...cheerfully willing."

"So Asia, are you saying that the word happy is overrated?" Wayne asked as he scratched his head. Sam grew worried that he reached Asia's wavelength.

"Exactly. The word is overrated and misunderstood. The state of being happy, however, is worthy of some serious respect." Asia smiled, pleased to know that someone could relate to her philosophy.

Rae just observed the conversation. *Boy she is weird*, he thought to himself. *God that just makes me love her even more.*

"Quite frankly, I think the dictionary's definition sucks." Sam stated as she followed Timmy into the kitchen.

Asia frustratingly brushed more hair out of her face, "What I'm saying is happiness is a choice. What I'm trying to prove is that many of us select exterior forces to satisfy something that should come from within."

Sam poked her head through the kitchen doorway, "so what are you saying that I could be happy without, let's say a good housekeeper?"

Asia nodded her head proudly, "precisely."

"And Lance could be happy if he ...let's say, chooses not to marry the woman of his dreams?" Sam asked as she walked back into the family room.

"Now you're getting it babe." Wayne stated.

"Don't you see Sam," Asia was getting philosophical, "people have got to create happiness from within."

Rae looked at her uncertain of where she was going with this thought.

"Rae, when I asked you, you responded 'you' to me. I appreciate it but I refuse to accept it."

"What do you mean?" Rae was offended.

"I love you, but I would never make you responsible for my happiness and I refuse to take responsibility for yours."

Rae was initially saddened but then it dawned on him where she was going and he nodded his head in agreement.

"That is the most unfair expectation one could place on another. Everyone should be responsible for themselves and their own happiness."

"I see what you are saying Asia but quite frankly, what is the point?" Sam questioned.

"I don't remember, but now I bet you will think twice when you are asked about what or who makes you happy."

Sam looked down, "I suppose you're right."

"That was my point." Asia gleefully added.

Rae hugged her and whispered in her ear, "you've always gotta have the last word, don't you."

Asia nodded, "always." She replied.

They all leaned back and pondered Asia's rant on happiness. They watched the fire blaze and cast a lovely light on their moment. If there was ever an exterior force to be thrilled about, it was this, being surrounded by people who loved each other, one could not ask for much better.

CHAPTER SEVEN
By My Side

IN THE DARK OF NIGHT, THOSE SMALL HOURS,
UNCERTAIN AND ANXIOUS, I NEED TO CALL YOU

Asia decided to sleep in. It was a lazy hot Saturday; she rolled over to find Rae typing away at the computer. "What are you working on?" She asked as she yawned.

"I told you it was a surprise."

Asia tilted her head to the side, remembering two weeks ago on the Vineyard, Rae telling her that he was working on a surprise. She yawned again and put her head back on the stack of pillows that surrounded the top of her bed. She snuggled close to a pillow and dreamt of what it was like to wake up alone. Since they returned from the Vineyard, Rae had slept over every night, even though the sex was still great, Asia felt like a part of her was fading away. The part that enjoyed being alone, the part that did not mind going to the movies alone or dining solo; the part of her that enjoyed rising when she felt like it, not because she was awakened. Rae was with her constantly, except when she was working, or he had a shoot.

"Honey," he was chipper and awake, "what are we doing today? I had this great idea of us going over to check out the new show at the Cinque Gallery, then doing lunch at this new place that Tim told me about, then..."

"Hey," Asia interrupted, "I have to go to my parents place and I'm sitting in for Carol tonight at the station."

Rae was taken aback by Asia's insensitivity. "Are you feeling okay, I mean did I do something wrong."

Asia pulled herself up. Ready to lie and tell Rae that everything was fine, but she really loved him and felt it was the perfect opportunity to be honest. "Rae, you know that I love you right?" She figured it would be a good idea to establish the positive big-picture first, men respond well to that sort of thing.

He nodded.

"Since we've come back from the Vineyard, I've been feeling kind of crowded, like we are spending too much time together." She paused then continued, "With us writing together, hanging out together, sleeping together and waking up together, I'm starting to feel a little lost, ya know?"

"No, I don't know." He stated quietly.

"Rae, let me ask you something." She brushed her hair out of her face, "Have you ever lived alone?"

"Well, I went away to college."

"But did you have a roommate?"

"Yes, but he was rarely there."

"That's not exactly what I'm talking about."

"So you mean, alone, alone?"

"Yes, that is what I mean."

"I suppose not, but what does that have to do with anything?"

"Rae, when I was growing up I always had my own everything, separate from Josh; my own room, my own bathroom, clothes, cars, everything. When I started graduate school, I moved in here, and I've been living alone since."

"So what are you saying, you want me to go?" He started to get upset.

Her head was aching; she massaged her temples as she spoke. "That is not what I'm saying at all, I'm trying to be honest with you. You see, I enjoy your company, but maybe you should start seeing your friends more or maybe stay at your place a few nights a week."

"Look Asia, if you want to know the truth, I was going to suggest that we move in together, but fuck it now." He got up in a frustrated huff.

"You also have to stop getting so damned upset when I'm being honest with you. Listen to me, don't read between my lines or make up shit as we go along. I just have to make sure that I maintain my own identity, I'm afraid of losing myself, or a part of me that is very special." Tears began to well up in her eyes. She was so pissed that she wanted to cry.

"To be so damned independent you cry an awful lot." He said in a sarcastic tone. "Quite frankly I find your demand for alone time to be selfish. You're so moody and selfish, just like all the other women I have been with."

Asia chuckled as she repeated him "Moody? Selfish? Did you ever think that your existence made them moody? Selfish? Motherfucker please you have been sitting up in my house, eating my food, using my shit and I am selfish? That's a joke." She felt it coming, the anger was about to explode through her body, and if she were not in her own place she would have thrown something by now.

"Oh please Asia, you know what else? You're a fucking liar."

"Me a liar? How in the hell did you come up with that one?"

He whined as he spoke "Because you told me you were not like everybody else, you said you were different from other women. You said you would never break my heart. And look what you're doing."

"Now!" She shouted.

He looked at her like she was insane. "Now what?" He asked.

She fixed her eyes on him and spoke through her firmly gritted teeth, "It's the time I want you to leave, that's what."

"So just like that?" He was confused.

"Yeah, just like that."

"Alright Asia tell me what's really on your mind."

"You are making me nuts, that's what's on my mind. I don't know if you're acting out one of your scripts with the shit you say or what. When I tell you what's really going on with me, you overlook it as if to say I am not being honest with you. Then you attack me because you don't like what it is I said." She was enraged. "Get out and you better go now before I ask you to never come back."

Rae shook his head and went to the bathroom to get dressed. He came out fully clothed saying nothing. She ignored him. She knew that if she looked at him she'd feel sick to her stomach. He left. Asia wondered why as soon as she got close to someone, she felt it necessary to push him away. But was she pushing him away or was she protecting herself?

He's too clingy, she thought to herself. *There is nothing worse than a clingy man. Fuck it, fuck him. I miss being alone anyway.*

She got out of bed and began to gather her dirty laundry to take to her parent's house. She stopped, noticing that she felt a sense of release, like the weight of the world was miraculously lifted off her shoulders. She realized that her headache was gone and so was Rae.

"Asia dear, you've got to realize that maybe you were meant to live alone." Rebecca Blake sipped her wine and glanced out the window as William frolicked in the back yard, about to cut the grass, then she lowered her voice, "trust me, I envy you. I wish I could live alone. Just enjoy it while you can, because if you ever do settle down, I'd hate to see you continue making the same mistake you always make."

"And what's that mom?" Asia asked blankly.

"You tend to dive head first into romantic situations, instead of putting one foot in the pool to test the climate."

Asia seemed surprised by her mother's observation, but she couldn't argue, she knew that her mother was right, as usual.

"But mom, that's my style, I was never a one foot in the pool type of girl."

"Then you will always wind up alone wondering what went wrong in your whirlwind romances. Look Asia, I know you are a person always in search for adventure and that's fine, but in the romance department, you need to listen to your inner voice more and take things slowly. This way you'll never have to worry about bailing out of a situation, when you go slowly you can bow out gracefully.

"But mom, the excitement of it all..."

"That's why romantic movies and novels are so successful, write about it. If you are lucky to live it, fine, but just remember, I've been married to your father for thirty years and he still never ceases to amaze me." She smiled and sipped her wine again. "And I'm still waiting for the proverbial happy ending."

"So damn, it's like that?" Asia shook her head. "So daddy, Josh, me, this house, is not your happy ending?"

"Damn girl," Rebecca paused, "please tell me you are not that foolish to believe that. I love you, Josh, your dad, this house, but this is hardly my happy ending. This would be my daddy's happy ending, for appearance sake, I have made it and that would have pleased him to see."

"So mom, what is your happy ending?"

"Baby when I figure that out, I will let you know."

"Well damn, I am half your age, if you don't know what it is, what in the hell am I searching for?"

"Perhaps that's your problem darling, you keep searching."

"Well mom what am I supposed to do just let it walk up and punch me in the face? Should I just stand there and wait?"

"No baby just live and do the best that you can. Use every day as the opportunity to do something that brings you joy, not search for it. Most importantly, do not search for it in a man."

William came in from going his yard work and planted a sweaty kiss on Rebecca's cheek. "Dinner ready baby?"

"Soon, go shower and then we will eat."

As William walked off he was mumbling something to Asia about getting him tickets to a fundraiser for Al Sharpton.

Asia thought of her conversation with her mother as she drove to the station. She thought of making a commitment to herself to take things slowly. *Mom's right, I really don't take the time to listen to myself.* She thought about her fight with Rae. She didn't feel bad or guilty, as far as she was concerned, whatever happens, happens. *No more stressing out, no more worrying. I'm just going to concentrate on living and being happy.*

Sam decided to take a cab home from the airport, she wanted to surprise Wayne. She was flying into Newark from Cleveland; her cousin jumped the broom that Friday night. When she called the airline and found out that there was an available seat on the Saturday evening flight, she jumped at it. She phoned him from her cellular while she was on the highway. "Hi honey, do ya miss me?"

He sounded like he was sleeping. "Yeah. When are you coming home?"

"Tomorrow morning was the soonest I could get."

"Do you need a ride?"

"Nope, I'm going to go right into the office and try to get some work done."

"Okay, well I'll see you tomorrow evening then."

She chuckled to herself. "Okay sweetie, see ya then."

The cab pulled up to the curb of the townhouse next door. She jumped out walked slowly to the door. She was wondering if she should enter the house quietly and strip before she climbed into bed with Wayne. She decided to just drop her bags and head to the bedroom. She entered quietly. All of the lights were out and the stereo in the living room was blasting Sade. Sam noticed that incense was burning and he had a few candles lit. She smiled. *So now I know he does the same thing as I do when I am home alone.* She thought to herself.

As she walked up the stairs, she heard the Jacuzzi running. She breathed a sigh of relief, knowing that he would not hear her. As she stepped into the bedroom, she heard Wayne's voice. Then she heard another man's voice yell "Oh yes big daddy, give it to me." Sam peeked into their bathroom and saw Wayne in the Jacuzzi with a man that looked familiar but she couldn't place the face. Her first reaction was to run into the bathroom and go off, she stopped herself.

She stepped back, and headed for Wayne's closet. She reached for his gun in the wooden case she gave him for his birthday. She quietly unloaded the chamber. She walked toward the bed and sat on the edge, she felt sick to her stomach. She took a deep breath and gained her composure.

Sam stood up and slowly walked into the bathroom, gun in hand. Wayne's bare ass high in the air, she sat on the toilet and as he happened upon a down stroke, she coolly said, "Honey, I'm home."

He instantly lost his erection at the sound of her voice. He stepped out of the tub. The man jumped up then leaned back into the Jacuzzi smirking.

"Sam, let me explain..."

"Oh shut the fuck up." She cut him off and pointed the gun at his penis. "I should shoot it off, but I may not be as lucky as Lorena Bobbitt."

The man in the Jacuzzi rose slowly and wrapped himself in towel as she and Wayne spoke.

Sam pointed the gun to the man in the tub, trying not to laugh, "Who the fuck are you?"

He shivered, "I'm Christian."

Sam was surprised at herself. She was calm and actually found the whole thing funny, she maintained a cool manner. "Yeah, the dude from the dry cleaners right?"

He nodded.

"Christian, give me back my towel, pick up your clothes and be the fuck out of my house before I count to ten. One!" Christian scurried off to gather his things. Sam turned back to Wayne. "You pitiful bastard can't even keep it up in a crisis." Her heart stopped when she noticed he was not wearing a condom.

"Um... I suggest you do the same as Christian."

"But Sam..."

She cut him off again, "don't you fucking dare say a word to me." She walked past him and headed for the window and opened it, she then went to his closet and pulled an arm-full of his clothes out and proceeded to throw them out of the window.

"Sam please stop, I... um..." He tried to pull her arm.

She snapped away from him and screamed "don't you ever put your filthy hands on me. Now get the fuck out." He just stood there. "Now!" She screamed at the top of her lungs. He pulled on a pair of sweatpants and stormed out of the house.

She followed him out and put the dead bolt and chain on the door. She headed to the den and leafed through the phone book. She dialed the number of a twenty-four hour locksmith. "Hi, when is the soonest I can have locks changed on my front and back doors?"

"Twenty minutes? Great. I'm at Society Mill in Upper Montclair, 16 Cliff Lane...and all I really need is to have the cores changed and money is no object...two-fifty, fine...do you take American Express? Great. I'll see you when you get here." She hung up the phone and broke out in tears.

———◆———

Cymone phoned Asia at the station to fill her in on Sam and Wayne. "Get the hell out of here." Is all Asia could say as Cymone went on with the sordid details "Wayne never struck me as the creeping type or the gay type."

Cymone puffed away on a cigarette. "Girl, you know those police officers are dogs."

"So how is she?"

"Unbelievably well, she's having her locks changed as we speak."

"Good, I'm glad she's at least thinking straight enough to take care of business. Damn, I'm still bugging off of this shit."

"What are you doing tomorrow?"

"I have nothing planned, why what's up?"

"I think we should go see Sam, maybe take her out for the day. Will Rae let us borrow you?"

Don't even get me started. I kicked him out of the loft this morning."

"What the fuck is going on here? What's wrong with you guys?"

"He got on my nerves and I asked him to go. I need my space.

"Here we go again."

"Oh Cymone, don't start. Listen, I might be able to swindle some Yankee tickets from my boss. Let's go to a game, drink some beer and have dinner in the city. That will get her mind off of things. We've got some sista girlfriend saving to do."

"Hey, I'm with it."

"Listen, I've got to get back to work, my intern is losing it. I get off at 12:00, and then I have to make an appearance at this new club downtown, before I go home. So buzz me in the morning after you've spoken to Sam."

Sam's eyes were swollen and her face looked sad and cold. When she answered the door to let Cymone and Asia in, she just mumbled "Hey", turned around and walked in a zombie like fashion, and plopped down on the sofa. Asia and Cymone followed her shaking their heads, recognizing that they have their work cut out for them.

The townhouse was a mess; Sam had all of Wayne's belongings in a huge pile in the middle of the floor.

"So what are ya going to do with these?" Cymone pointed to the pile.

"At first I thought about burning them," Sam spoke as if she were an empty shell. There was no emotion in her tone or gestures "but I figured I wouldn't waste my time."

Asia got up from the sofa across from Sam, sat beside her, and took her hand. "Sam, we're worried about you. Do you want to talk about it?"

Sam's lovely round face was accented with a Toni Braxton-esque haircut. She gently leaned back and snuggled to one of the tapestry pillows on her over-sized leather sofa. She raised her sad eyes to Asia and quietly said, "I'm okay, and I really don't want to speak on it. Not now, I just want to be... live... ya know?"

Cymone lit a cigarette. "Listen Sam, if you don't want to talk about it, we understand but there is no way we're going to leave you here by yourself, so go upstairs, put on some shoes, throw on some shades and let's be out of here."

Makin' Happy

"Cymone is right Sam. We are worried about you, and we know that if we left you here," Asia got up and headed to the huge showcase window and raised the blinds, "you'd sit around here with the place all dark and dreary." She walked to the kitchen and opened the blinds in the kitchen. The sunlight came steaming in, it made Sam squint.

Sam covered her eyes, "Damn, I didn't realize that the sun was out."

Asia walked around the townhouse raising every blind, tying back every curtain. She bounced back down the stairs and said "Come on girl," she glanced at the Rolex her mother gave her for graduation and continued, "time is a wasting; the boys in pinstripes await us."

As Asia raced up Route 80, Cymone told jokes, trying to make Sam laugh. Nothing worked until Asia pulled a blunt out of her sunglasses case. "It's time for a little something Rae left behind."

Cymone shook her head. "Damn Asia, I thought you gave that shit up."

"Hey, drastic times call for drastic measures." Asia smiled, leaned over and popped in Queen Latifah's Black Reign Cassette.

Sam took the blunt from Asia and lit it. "I have not touched this stuff since we were in Atlanta. But hey, I'm free and from now on I'm gonna do whatever the fuck I want."

"You know," Sam spoke in a lazy drunken tone, "Men ain't shit." She took a long hard drag from the blunt. She continued, "Not to say that I blame all them mother fuckers for what Wayne did but damn, can't a sister get a fuckin' break?"

"P..l..e..a..s..e.." Asia responded in her Miles Davis cool motherfucker voice, "a break? You wanna break? The only break you can expect is your heart or your wallet."

"Now listen, as far as I'm concerned the heart is the only thing that is an option." Cymone soberly chimed in. "He can have my heart but the money is under serious lock and key, I've worked too hard for some fool to clean me out. But don't fuck it up; sex is more important in a relationship than money, as far as I'm concerned."

Asia cleared her throat, "that's true, 'cause a man with a lot of money and a little dick ain't shit."

"Can I get a witness?" Sam screamed imitating her father who was preacher. They all laughed and jammed to "Coochie Bang".

Asia whipped her Jeep up to the Bronx. She decided to park close to the stadium and just pay extra. They needed beer and they needed it quick. This was no time for her usual to walk from Harlem and across the Macombs Dam Bridge.

Yankee stadium was crowded as usual. Asia loved the fans as much as the team itself. "They are so lively, so loud, and so much fun." She sipped her beer and screamed "Go Yankees, kick that ass!!!"

Sam looked at Asia and Cymone and forced a smile, "thanks a lot you guys; I'm really having a great time." She lied.

Asia entered the loft quietly as if she were sneaking in. *What am I doing? I'm alone.* She thought to herself. "I think I'm going to get a dog, I need to have something around here loyal, and that doesn't argue with me and is happy to see me every time I walk through the door..." Her solo conversation was cut short by the ringing of the telephone.

She lazily strutted to the sofa, plopped down, and reached for the phone, "hello?"

"Hi, it's me," Rae's voice was monotone.

"Hey Rae, what's up?" Asia immediately felt the tension headache building.

"I miss you, that's what's up. Are you still mad?"

"Rae, I'm not mad but I just got in and I have a splitting headache. Can I call you later?"

"Sure." He said nastily and hung up.

"Damn." Asia sighed and closed her eyes. Within five minutes, her headache was gone. She reached for the phone and called Cymone.

"Yo Cy, have you ever heard of someone making someone else physically ill?"

Cymone chuckled, "hell yeah, my principal makes me sick every day."

"No for real, I was feeling fine, then Rae called...boom! Splitting headache, when I hung up it went away."

"Sounds like bad karma girlfriend."

Asia's call waiting clicked in. "All right girl, I was just tripping. I'll talk to you tomorrow." Asia clicked over "Yeah?"

"You are such a spoiled bitch I can't believe the way you treat me sometimes." Rae yelled into the phone.

"I refuse to get into this with you Rae; don't start this shit with me." Asia slammed down the phone. *That is it I've fucking had it.* Asia thought to herself. *No more men!* She jumped up off the sofa and went straight to the window. The sun had just set and the sky was a gorgeous shade of purple. She lit a cigarette. "Am I going to be alone forever?" She exhaled. "Is that such a bad thing?" She headed for the computer and decided to write down how she was feeling.

That was the problem, not finding a man, but finding a companion whom she could share her feelings with. That was foreign to Asia. She thought of all her past relationships. Devin popped in her mind first. He was kind, but there was no real communication going on, except when they were angry. Asia wondered why it was so easy to communicate anger, but the other stuff, connecting on a level deeper than just the physical, which was the hard part.

Greg. What a mess that turned into. Like a lightning bolt her mind went to her conversation with Lance. Asia realized what "it" was. Intimacy. Something that all of her relationships lacked. It's not money. For if you lost everything, that person would be right there, by your side.

It wasn't sex, for great sex and an empty relationship is a stepping-stone towards disaster.

Intimacy and respect. Mix that with a heavy dose of positive, constant communication, and you have the foundation of a lasting relationship. *So maybe I won't swear them off, I'll just be a lot more careful and focused on what is important.*

Sam knew she was depressed. She took a week off from work and stayed in bed the entire time. It had been a month since she caught Wayne. Every day she felt sicker and sicker. Her hair began to fall out and she lost fifteen pounds. The worst of it all, she hadn't heard from Wayne. She sat at her desk and daydreamed. Tina, her assistant entering her office, startled her.

"Oh, I'm sorry Ms. Carlin." Tina whispered. "Are you okay?"

Sam shook her head and cleared her voice. "Yes, I'm fine."

Tina approached Sam's desk and placed a business card in front of her. She gently said, "Here, this is my doctor." She stopped and bit her lip; "she helped me a great deal when I lost my mom. She mixes holistic and western medicine focusing on women, their issues and how they deal with it. She's a therapist and MD all rolled into one."

Sam took a deep breath trying to hold back a tear. "Thank you" she whispered.

Tina quietly left the office and Sam read the card, recognizing that something had to change and reached for the phone.

Makin' Happy

Sam tossed and turned; it had been three days since her visit to Tina's doctor. The blood work was due in this morning. She looked at the alarm clock. 6:00 AM. She didn't fall asleep till 4:00. She forced herself out of bed and to the shower. She dragged as she put on her clothes and makeup. She forced herself to take a bite out of a piece of toast. She had no appetite. She stared at the bottle of Seconal the doctor had prescribed for her insomnia; she had refused to take any, feeling that she can combat her problem alone.

Sam walked out of the doctor's office in a daze. She got into her car and headed straight to the airport. She had no emotion, she was lifeless. She drove past her office building without giving it a glance.

She parked the car at the airport and headed straight to Delta ticketing center. "Hello." she said in a sad, deep melodic voice. From behind her dark glasses, she spoke to the agent. "Please book me for the next one-way flight you have to Arizona...Phoenix, and please make it first class." She placed her American Express Platinum card on the counter.

"Yes Ma'am." The clerk punched a few buttons and he quickly responded. "We have a flight departing at 1:35, boarding time is in fifty minutes and first class is available. Will you be checking any luggage?"

"No." Sam said quietly.

Would you need a rental car while you are there?"

"Yes." Sam said quietly, "make it something luxuriously satisfying in a convertible."

The clerk wasted no time. "Well ma'am, Hertz has a Saab convertible and a Jaguar convertible."

"I'll take the Jag." Sam sighed as she took back her American Express card. She smiled as the clerk handed her the ticket.

"Have a nice trip ma'am." The clerk smiled and gave her the regular closing speech as if he were a machine.

Sam walked to the gate and sat in front of the huge window overlooking the runway. She pulled out her cellular phone and called American Express Travel Services.

"Ah...yes, this is Samantha Carlin." Sam gave the travel agent her account number and made a reservation for the Camel Back Inn and Spa in Phoenix, for two nights. She placed her telephone and checked to make sure her Seconal was in her bag. She put on her sunglasses and stood when boarding for her flight was announced. She boarded the plane sat down and sighed again. "I'm going out in style," she said to herself under her breath.

Sam arrived in Phoenix refreshed from her nap on the plane and she felt amazingly focused. As she drove to the spa, she thought back to a conversation she had with Asia and Cymone. They were all watching television when, on November 7, 1991, the emergency news report informed them of Magic Johnson being diagnosed with HIV.

"Get the fuck out of here." Asia gasped as she spoke. "Damn, I've loved Magic since I was a kid. They can't be serious."

Cymone and Sam sat in silence as they listened to the report.

"Asia jumped up, and grabbed a cigarette and dragged on it. She looked at Sam and Cymone in disbelief. "They can't be serious. Magic? No, not Magic!"

"Just goes to show you, "Cymone looked at Asia and Sam, "AIDS hits everybody." She paused. "You know, I try to tell my students that all the time. When I hear of another one getting pregnant, it makes me cringe. I hope they realize that pregnancy is the best thing that could come out of that situation. Shit I'm a single mother, with a job…a good job and I have a rough time with Brianna, but at least I was out of college and working when I had her. They don't even learn from the ordeal, kids are dropping off left and right from this disease."

Sam spoke as she looked at the television. "I thought it was a gay, drug addict thing."

"Oh, come on Sam, you can't be for real." Asia was surprised at Sam's conservative viewpoint. "AIDS can hit anybody, look; it's going to get Magic."

"Damn Sam, don't you watch these talk shows?" Cymone said surprised. "Everybody is getting it; it's just that no one takes notice till something like this happens."

"You know what the fucked up thing is?" Asia chuckled in bewilderment, "If I had met him, I would have fucked him. Like almost any other woman and I would have been caught up in the star fucker thing, ya know? Not even thinking about...or even considering the possibility that I could die from such an encounter."

Cymone decided to take the conversation further to the frightening level. What would you do if you were diagnosed with HIV?"

"Good question." Asia spoke as if she were in a trance. "I think I would go straight to my mother and talk to her. She is the one person who I could cry to and she can help me make sense out of the most fucked up situation." Asia dragged her cigarette and continued, "Then I'd probably go to the GMHC and try to get counseling and try to connect with and help people like me, suffering with the same problem. What about you Cymone, what would you do if you were diagnosed?"

"Well, suicide would probably be a consideration. Then I'd come to my senses and make sure that Brianna was fine and going to be taken care of." Cymone thought for a moment, "I think that it would be important for her to be able to understand that her mommy would be living with HIV and possibly AIDS, not dying from it. What about you Sam?"

Sam stared at the floor for a while before she spoke. "I'd kill myself, plain and simple."

"What?" Asia questioned in horror. "Surely, you can't mean that Sam."

"For real." Sam shook her head and spoke easily, "I wouldn't go out of that type of situation any other way. I'd fly away to somewhere I had never been, somewhere nice and peaceful. Then I'd check into a fancy hotel and do it right there. First class all the way. I could never bear with explaining to my father that I was diagnosed with the devil's disease. My daddy is a preacher; I couldn't embarrass him and my mother like that."

Asia and Cymone just looked at Sam in shock.

God damn, what do you say to somebody after they told you some deep shit like that? Asia thought to herself. She just folded her arms to give herself warmth after the chill of Sam's voice coursed up her spine.

The wind blew seductively through Sam's hair as she drove to the spa. She held her head up high and for the first time in months she had energy. She felt like she could run five miles. She turned on the radio and War was crooning "Life Is So Strange". She thought of Wayne as she nodded her head to the beat.

She followed the bellhop to her suite. Tipped him twenty dollars and drew a hot bath. She lay in the tub still focused and energized while sipping seven glasses of champagne. She knew that there was no place she'd rather be and no way she'd rather go."

She pulled herself gently from the tub and carefully dried her body, as if she were handling a fine piece of crystal. She headed for the bed and poured herself a glass of water. She laid out the some thirty odd pills she had on the nightstand. She decided it would be easier to swallow them in small groups as opposed to one at a time.

After swallowing her last group she placed her head on the pillow and gently closed her eyes. As she drifted off to sleep, visions of her childhood passed through her mind. Before she drifted to her demise, "First class all the way...so Daddy will never know." echoed in her mind.

CHAPTER EIGHT

Bitter Tears

IN THE MIST OF MY ENDLESS SEARCH, THE BEST IN LIFE BECOMES CLEAR, THE REST JUST BEGINS TO FADE BY ITSELF

Asia and her producer Yeva chatted and toked on a pack of cigarettes filling the lounge with smoke.

"Yeah girl "Yeva continued, "men were never my cup of tea, Celeste and I have been together for three years. Did I tell you we just put a down payment on the house of our dreams?"

"Wow Yeva that's great, where?"

"Montclair, taxes are high but we feel it's worth every penny."

"Did you set the date for the commitment ceremony yet?"

"No date has been set; we are going to wait till we move in, probably around the holidays."

Ted, the receptionist poked his head in the door, "Excuse me Asia, you have an urgent call on two."

"Thanks Ted, I'll take it in here." As Asia walked to the phone, she felt like she was in a tunnel and the phone seemed so far away, her ears went deaf, as if she were underwater every step she took was in slow motion, like in a dramatic scene in film, she knew something was wrong, in that very instant, she knew that all was not right and lifted the receiver "Asia Blake here."

"Asia?" Cymone sobbed as she spoke. "We need to talk right away, it's Sam."

"What is it Cy?"

"I'd rather tell you in person, can you get Yeva to cover you?"

"Yes, do you want me to come to your place?"

"No, my mom is here with Bri, I'll meet you at the loft."

"Okay I'll be there in a half an hour. Okay?"

"Good, and Asia, be careful." Cymone hung up.

"Yeva, there has been an emergency, can you cover for me tonight? Asia began to tremble; she knew it in that instant that Sam was gone.

"Sure Asia, just go, I'll take care of everything."

"Thanks Yeva, I'll call you later." Asia raced out of the studio and drove quickly to Jersey, Cymone's car was in the garage."

Asia entered the apartment to find Cymone sitting on the sofa in the dark, drinking a glass of wine. Asia sat beside her and put her arm around her.

"She did it A, she went and did it."

"Did what?"

Cymone sighed and spoke slowly, "Sam's father called me this evening, she's gone A, she's really gone."

Tears streamed down Asia's face, "What happened Cymone, what did he say?"

"She was found dead in a suite at a spa in Phoenix. She was found in her room about 4:00 PM our time…she…she overdosed on sleeping pills."

Asia clenched her fist and banged it on the couch, "that Wayne idiot drove her to this. She was depressed, why couldn't we see it? We could have saved her."

"No Asia, not exactly, don't you see? She must have been HIV positive, which was why she lost all of that weight."

"What would make you think of that? If Sam was HIV positive, she would have told us, right?"

"Asia, don't you remember that night we found out Magic was HIV positive?"

"Oh, damn." Asia whispered.

"She told us then," Cymone sobbed heavily, "she said that she would kill herself 'in style' so her family would never know."

"Do you really think that Sam killed herself in a spa, because she was HIV positive?"

"I'd feel chillingly safe saying that is exactly what she did. "Look," Cymone wiped her face and sat up looking as if she were mad, speaking quickly as if she were solving a murder mystery, "her father told me she flew first class to Phoenix, just leaving the office, not even telling her secretary where she was going. She rented a fucking Jaguar convertible, drove to one of the most expensive spas there and left no note, nothing."

"Damn, why didn't she say anything? We could have helped her"

"Asia, realistically, what could we possibly have done?"

Asia's mind raced, *we could have talked with her, helped her through it*, she thought. A feeling of terrifying doom took over her, realizing there was nothing she or anyone else could have done. "I suppose you are right Cymone."

"So what now?" Cymone asked.

"Well let's call her folks and ask them if they need any help. I think we should go to her place and go through her stuff before her parents do."

"I already spoke with her sisters; they said that they would go through her townhouse." Cymone lit a cigarette. "I think Stacey was due to arrive from Durham today, she will actually be staying there a few weeks. Heather left her parents house and headed straight to Sam's after she heard the news. I asked her if she wanted us to help her, and she thought it would be best if she and Stacey started alone."

Asia pondered on how devastated they must feel. God I can't even begin to imagine what I would do if something happened to Josh." She wiped the tears from her face and reached for the telephone. "We better call Lance and Charla and let them know."

The funeral service was beautiful. It made Asia think a lot about life, her relationships with family, friends and forced her to put things into the proper perspective. While following the limousine, Asia sang along with Bob Marley's "No Woman No Cry". Tears streamed down her face. *Damn Sam, why did you have to go there?* She thought to herself, *just know that I love ya girlfriend.* As she drove to the cemetery, she lit a joint. She pulled on it deeply. She exhaled with sort of a sigh of relief. *I have my guardian angel now, watch over me Sam, I'm going to need you.* When she arrived to the grave site, she dropped a few drops of Visine in her eyes, popped a piece of gum in her mouth, touched up her lipstick, and put on her sunglasses and headed to the burial. She walked up behind Cymone who was weeping silently.

"Hey girl," Asia grabbed her hand.

Cymone squeezed Asia's hand, "Hey."

"Cy, you okay?"

"Part of me is so angry with her for not telling us how much pain she was in. The other part is angry with myself for not knowing, not doing anything to help her." She whispered.

"Cymone, there was nothing that we could do, she took risks, she was privy to all of the same information we were. Stop feeling guilty, you knew the deal, she told us," Asia paused and looked around to make sure that no one would hear them. "There still would have been nothing we could have done for her."

"You know while I was at her folks house last night, her mother looked me in the eye and said 'Cymone, why would my baby do this to herself?'" Cymone squeezed Asia's hand harder. "I just

Makin' Happy

looked her in the face and cried. Her parents think that she was depressed about the breakup with Wayne."

"Well, I know it may not be right, but we have to respect Sam's wishes, she would rather have her parents think that, rather than knowing the truth. Besides, we can only assume that she was…you know." Asia hugged Cymone.

As the last words were spoken and tears fell, Asia felt a tug at her heart that Sam got exactly what she wanted, a first class passing with dignity and no one knowing exactly why.

Lance, Charla, Asia, and Cymone returned to Asia's loft after the burial. Charla constantly rubbed her belly. The passing of Sam made her gain a new appreciation for the life growing inside of her. She no longer resented her baby for taking over her body.

They all sat around the coffee table and with sad eyes and heavy hearts. Asia went to the kitchen and emerged holding glasses, a corkscrew and a bottle. Asia placed the glasses on the table and handed the bottle of Glen Ellen to Lance and told him to open it. She ran to her bedroom and reached in the back of her closet, to a little black purse. She unzipped it and pulled out a sock, she gently unpacked a little glass bong and she blew the dust off of it. She stopped in her bathroom to fill it with water, and went back into the living room and plopped down on an over sized pillow, just next to Charla. She reached across the coffee table to grab a heart shaped box with pre-crushed weed in it and began to pack the bowl. She knew she needed something to shake off her sadness. She needed to discuss something positive; Sam would have wanted it to be that way.

"So Lance and Charla, are you all ready to make that move?" Asia asked as she sipped a glass of wine.

"Six weeks and counting" Charla replied. Lance sat quietly and rubbed her shoulders.

"I think we need to talk about it, her" Cymone blurted out. "We can't just sit here like nothing has happened and not speak on it or on her." Cymone began to sob uncontrollably.

"Okay Cy, I will start." Asia blew out a cloud of smoke after taking a long hit on the bong. "Let me just say here and now that I loved Sam. She was an amazing woman. She gave so much to this world and she took so much away from it, when she took her own life." Asia sipped her wine and tears streamed down her face. "I loved her then, I love her now and I always will."

"Let us raise our glasses to that." Lance said as he lifted his glass.

They all clanked their glasses and sipped.

"I remember when I met Sam at one of your sorority functions." Charla chimed in. "She made me feel right at home, and ever since then I knew we would be friends. I know she is in a better place, with the Lord. Her beautiful spirit and smile will never be forgotten." Charla motioned to hold her glass in the air and they all cheered again. "To Samantha"

"To Samantha" they all repeated.

Cymone blew out a stream of smoke after hitting the bong. She solemnly spoke. "Sam and I grew up together. She was my best friend and my confidant. She always brought sunshine to my cloudy days. She was the first person I spoke to about everything, my period, sex, my first love, my pregnancy." Cymone sipped her wine and continued as the tears streamed down her face. "She will always be in my heart and I know that her spirit is with us."

"To Samantha" Asia whispered as she held her glass up. Everyone else raised their glasses in silence.

The bells of the Basilica chimed on the glorious October morning as the white Rolls Royce Bentley limousine pulled up. The leaves were swirling in the warm breeze and the sun beamed. Asia and Charla sat in the back seat, as the other bride's maids were in the traditional stretch Cadillac behind them. Asia was Charla's maid of honor and her eyes welled up with tears at the sight of her cousin in her lovely white chiffon gown. Charla embraced her belly with her left hand and held Asia's hand tightly with her right.

They watched the final guests arrive and scurry to the inside.

"Are you ok honey?" Is all Asia could say. "I know you are getting tired of me asking you that but you're my cousin, no fuck that, you're my sister, and I love you. It is my responsibility to make sure you are ok today."

"Asia, I appreciate it, I," she paused and glanced at her belly, "we are fine. Just ready to make this official."

Asia reached into her purse and pulled out a compact of MAC translucent powder. She opened it and checked her lipstick in the mirror and then pulled a brush out of her bag, dabbed the brush in the powder, and began to gently brush Charla's face. "You look simply magnificent my dear."

Charla began to get tears in her eyes. "Thank you. I wish Sam was here today."

Asia looked up to the sky and said, "She is here. I feel her smiling down on you."

Asia spotted the wedding coordinator exiting the church and motioning for them to come in. "Moment of truth are you ready to go in there and marry my boy?" She asked.

Charla beamed "hell yeah!"

Asia ushered Charla into the church as her father stood there in utter pride at the beauty of his daughter. Asia walked up and kissed him on the cheek "Hey Uncle Paul, you are looking handsome in that tux."

"Thank you Asia" he hugged her and then headed for Charla.
"You ready princess?"
"Yes daddy I am ready" Charla winked at Asia.

As Asia marched down the long isle, to Pachelbel's Cannon, she thought of Sam, and felt a warm feeling that she was there, watching. She locked eyes with Cymone, looking as if she were thinking the same thing about Sam. They smiled lovingly toward each other. She fixed her eyes on Lance, standing elegantly and proudly, riddled with emotion and accomplishment. Brianna was a perfect flower girl gently tossing white and red rose petals down the aisle.

As Cannon came to a stop, the crowd rose and turned toward the back where Charla was to make her entrance. The organ hit the first four notes of "Here Comes the Bride" and the doors opened. Asia's eyes welled up with tears the moment her eyes connected with Charla's. She knew that if two people were ever made for each other it was Charla and Lance. She glanced at Lance who bit his bottom lip as his eyes were fixed on Charla, with a stream of tears flowing. There was not a dry eye in the wedding party by the time Charla made it to the altar.

Asia thought to herself *If this chick was not my cousin I would want to beat her ass. She got the guy and she got the life. All by being her sweet simple self.* It made her feel some sense of pleasure knowing that if anyone had to get the happily ever after, it should be Charla.

After the vows and rings were exchanged the bridal parties headed to their respective limousines. The men had their own stretch, the ladies, their own, and Lance and Charla lead the way in the Rolls. The wedding party was whisked away to take photographs in a park in Bergen County. On the ride, Asia and Cymone cracked open a bottle of Champagne and laughed at the lack of single and attractive friends Lance had. Asia tried to ignore the fact that Jay was in attendance, with his new fiancé. She was Jewish and ultimately Asia was sure that is what he really wanted.

The reception was large, lavish in traditional Lance and Charla style; there was an overflow of top shelf food, liquor and happy faces dancing into the night.

Makin' Happy

Asia sat on the dais and thought to herself as to why in her late twenty's she was yet again a bride's maid and not a bride. She watched the couples dance to Dinah Washington's "Fly Me to the Moon", the older couples; William and Rebecca included, swayed, dipped, smooched, and shook their shoulders when the pace picked up. Asia watched Lance and Charla stay in their trance like sway as the older folks partied. Then the Disc Jockey changed the tone completely. The old folks scurried away from the dance floor and the younger attendees crowded the floor. "Makin' Happy" by Crystal Waters pumped and blared through the speakers. Asia started grooving and looked to Cymone who was hugged up with Timmy on the dance floor. She mouthed to Cymone "This is my jam" and proceeded to the dance floor.

Asia was in the middle of the floor with her arms high in the air and she sang and spun to the song. It was like she was in a world all her own, just she and the music. At that moment she decided that she was no longer going to be over consumed with why she was not the bride. She made a note to herself to congratulate Jay and his new love, for she really was happy for him. This would be her theme song she thought, she would dance, drink, smoke, and make happy for the rest of her life.

The sun was streaming through Asia's window. It was a brisk November morning. Asia reached for the phone to call Josh at school.

"Hey, little brother"

"What up sis?"

"Just wanted to know if you were coming home for the holiday?" Asia felt sad. She wanted to cry. Her emotions were running high since Sam's funeral and Charla's wedding.

"So how did it go? The funeral."

"It was sad and very intense."
"Are you okay?"
"Yes Josh, I'm fine, just missing you"
"Miss ya too sis. Listen I've got a class. I need to get moving"
"Okay I don't want to hold you up, just wanted to say hey and see what was up for the Holiday. Do you need me to pick you up at the airport?"
"Nah, one of my girls is picking me up."
"K babe, I'll see you in a few weeks."
"Peace."

Asia got out of bed and walked over to the computer and turned it on. She wanted to write, but felt nothing. After staring at her cursor blinking on a blank page, she decided that getting out and doing some Christmas shopping would be the thing to do. She just wanted to lose herself and blend in with a crowd of unknown faces. As she shopped she thought of taking a vacation. She made a mental note to herself to ask her mom if she could use the timeshare in Aruba.

She dug out her cell phone from her pocketbook and called her mother to secure the timeshare. "But Asia, the flights are ridiculous during the Christmas season." Her mother warned. "Especially waiting so late to book."

"Mom, I really need to do this, I really don't care how much it will cost."

"At least you don't have to worry about paying for a place to stay. Okay, I will call the Suites and let them know that you will be arriving on the twenty-sixth."

"Thanks mom, I appreciate it."

"Oh don't worry; I'm just glad that you have the time to enjoy it. Lord knows your father and I are way too busy to travel right now."

"Thanks again mom, I love you"

"And I you dear."

Asia quickly called her travel agent to shop for flights. She called Asia back with the quotes. She booked a flight for two.

Asia dialed Cymone's number.

"Hey Brianna, how are you?"

"Auntie Asia! Hey guess what? I'm getting straight A's for the first marking period."

"Oh boy, you are going to break me."

"That's right, you said one dollar for every A" Brianna started to giggle. "Hold on I will get mommy for you…. Mommy!!!"

Cymone picked up the phone sounding winded. "Hey girl."

"What are you doing?"

"Tae Bo girl, Billy Blanks is whipping my tail. So what's up?"

"Picture this, me, you, Aruba…the week after Christmas. Can you hang?"

"Damn, how much is it going to cost me?"

"Eight Fifty, all you need is airfare; I'll take care of everything else. You down?"

"Well I gotta see if Mommy will keep Brianna. It sounds like a great idea."

"Yes it does, come on Cy, we owe it to ourselves to take a trip and get spiritually centered." Asia was getting excited. She needed spiritual renewal.

"Let me talk to my mom and I'll call you back in a few."

"Sounds good." Asia hung up the phone and lit several candles around the room. She turned off all of the lights and began to meditate. Her session was interrupted by Cymone's message; she turned the ringer off but forgot to lower the volume on the machine.

"Yo girlie, it's on, Mom will keep Brianna. Call me back with the details, peace."

Asia smiled to herself and went back to chanting.

Asia reflected on Thanksgiving dinner as she drove to the station. The Jeep was reeking of turkey and trimmings as her mom packed plates for Asia to take to the station for Yeva and the rest of the crew. She chuckled to herself as she thought of Josh and his girlfriend. She was a typical Morristown black bourgeoisie, tall, thin, pretty, and daughter of a prominent husband and wife doctor team. Jack and Jill alumnus and a freshman at Colby.

Asia jammed to The Fugees as she drove into the city. She smiled as she thought of her upcoming trip to Aruba. "Oh la la la la la la la la la la it's a we thing…"

Asia walked into the station. She loved working on holiday nights. The station was low key and outside of a few office folks manning the phones, it was just she, Yeva and the crew.

Yeva was sitting in the lounge finishing up a conversation on the phone. "Hey Asia, I'll be right with you."

Yeva went back to her conversation. "Yeah, okay. But why so damned late? Um hum. Okay love, I'll make arrangements to get him. See ya soon. Love you too. Bye."

Yeva hung up the phone and sauntered over to Asia. She was glowing. Being in love agreed with her. She was a shapely size 18, with light brown skin and chestnut colored eyes. Her brown hair was in locks. She was a beautiful, smart woman. Asia loved to watch the men that approached her clutch their hearts as they walked away wounded. Never having a shot at the zaftig beauty. She was in love. She and Celeste were having their commitment ceremony the following Saturday.

"Asia, what are you doing tonight after the show?"

"Oh I don't know. I'm just gonna head home I guess. No club appearances tonight thank God. I'm getting too old for that shit. Why what's up?"

"Celeste's cousin is flying in from Maine. He's coming into LaGuardia. Would you mind driving me to the airport to pick him up?"

"Sure what the hell."

Makin' Happy

"He's spending time with us and helping us get things together for the big day."

The telephone rang in the lounge, Asia answered it. "Hello? Oh hi. Sure she's right here. Hold on." Asia passed the phone to Yeva, "It's your cousin in-law Spencer."

Yeva grabbed the phone; "Thanks babe…Spence, what time is the flight? And the number? Okay got it; well I can't get there till about one, one-thirty. So why don't you just have a drink while you are waiting? Cool. I'll see you then, yes the usual spot…Yes…Yes it is…Yes she is…Well you will get to meet her, she is coming with me. Okay, bye bye."

Asia grabbed her bottle of water and headed toward the studio, Yeva followed. "So is cousin Spencer gay?"

"No not at all why would you ask that?"

"Well, his voice was a bit high, soft and breathy"

"Girl he is far from gay."

"Married?"

"Nope. And he's got a good job. He's a jazz musician and a Music Professor at University of Maine."

"Interesting, a brother from Maine."

"Maine via Harlem"

Asia sat at the board as Yeva got situated at her booth to begin the countdown. While the promo was playing Yeva came up on the intercom and said "Oh yeah, brother is fine too. And five, four, three…."

Asia smiled and shook her head.

The ride to the airport was a quick one but getting back across the bridge was a nightmare, the usual after midnight construction on the GWB was in full effect. Spencer fell asleep as soon as they exited the airport. Asia looked back at him in the rearview mirror. *How sweet* she thought.

He snored like he was sawing trees. She and Yeva laughed at him as he slept.

CHAPTER NINE

Never Tear Us Apart

I, I WAS STANDING, YOU WERE THERE, TWO WORLDS COLLIDING, AND THEY COULD NEVER TEAR US APART

Asia and Cymone attended the Commitment Ceremony together. Yeva and Celeste wore beautiful matching evening dresses. The house was decorated in lilies and rainbows. Asia leaned over to Cymone during the reception.

"So what do you think about Celeste's cousin Spencer?"

Cymone chewed her salad hungrily and responded, "He's cute, not my type though."

"Cymone," Asia was perplexed, "What is your type?"

"Girl if I knew that, we'd be at my wedding!"

They both laughed. Spencer walked over to their table and sat down next to Asia.

"So what did you think?" He spoke in his soft breathy voice.

"It was absolutely beautiful, I cried" Asia turned to him. *His voice is so soft, he sounds like he's gay* she thought.

He chuckled. "I noticed."

"Do I have mascara streaks?"

Spencer took the handkerchief out of his suit pocket and gently rubbed it across Asia's face. "There all better now."

Asia smiled. "Thanks…So when do you head back?"

"Tomorrow, my students have a big holiday concert and we have got to rehearse."

"Nice." Asia nervously smiled. She turned back to Cymone. "Cy this is Spencer Barksdale. Spencer, this is Cymone Grant."

Cymone gave a phony smile. "Charmed."

Spencer looked back at Asia and asked, "Can I get you a drink?"

"Sure, red wine please."

Asia's eyes followed him as he walked to the bar. *Cute* she thought. *Nice body good teeth, bald and bulky just how I like 'em.* Spencer placed the wine in front of her and reached out his hand. He escorted Asia to the kitchen. Yeva and Celeste's kitchen was fabulous, huge and airy. The caterers were busily working. "Let's go to the study, it's a bit too active in here." He smiled as he led her to the small den off from the kitchen. He sat Asia down on the love seat and pulled up the chair that was in front of the computer desk. "So Asia, tell me about yourself." He smiled and leaned back.

"Well, I'm a struggling writer, my first book was pretty successful in this market, my second book is soon to be released, but I've been working on a sitcom treatment and I have a great idea for a film. I'm just in a bit of a rut, afraid that I may spread myself too thin." Asia felt a bit uncomfortable, his eyes were steady and focused; she wasn't used to brothers with so much intensity. "So Yeva tells me you are a Jazz musician, what's your instrument?"

"Piano, but I was classically trained. I broke into jazz while in grad school as an outlet and to make a little loot."

"Cool."

"Do you listen to classical music?"

"Not really, I have a few favorites but I'm not a huge follower, popular music is more my thing."

"So how do you like being a deejay?"

"It's great, the money could be better but it affords me the opportunity to work on my writing."

"I'd like to read some of your stuff sometime, if you don't mind"

"Only if I get to hear you play."

He flashed a broad smile, "It's a deal."

"So Spencer, tell me, what's a handsome brother like you doing in Maine?"

He blushed and smiled. "Thank you. Well I went to grad school there and never left. I was lucky enough to be offered a job right after I graduated."

"Lucky you." Asia laughed. "I raised so much hell in grad school, they were only too happy to show me the door when I left. I was the loud mouth at every rally, either fighting for students rights or an ousted professor's tenure."

"I can't imagine you starting up trouble." He smiled at her, licking his lips in that sexy LL Cool J sort of way.

"I've mellowed out quite a bit." Asia paused. "So what do you do when you are not making music?"

"Well I fish...I love to fish." He smiled as his mind drifted at the idea of fishing, it had been a while, winter started pretty early this year. "Do you fish?"

Asia was surprised and thought to herself; *fish? Hell I don't have the patience for that...*"No, I don't fish, but I swim, love to swim, how about you?"

He shook his head, "The only stroke I know is the dead man's float."

Suddenly Asia started to feel like any semblance of a connection was out the window. "So how about museums and art do you enjoy art?"

"Not really, I'm not a big fan of museums." He suddenly blurted out "I want to tell you about my mother, she..."

Asia paused and attempted to act as if she was interested in him but she had already seen red, a red flag that is. *Why in the hell is he talking to me about his mother?* She thought. Trying not to be rude, when he finished his momma bit, she excused herself to go to the restroom. When she came out of the restroom, she spotted Cymone sitting alone sipping wine; she motioned for her to come join her. They locked the bathroom door and devised a plan that Cymone did not feel well, and leaving immediately was the best option.

Asia went back to the study and apologized to Spencer, explaining that she had to leave early to take Cymone home. He was cool about it and offered to walk them to the car. Asia started "I was very nice meeting you Spencer. I am going away in a few weeks for vacation, but how about if I give you a buzz when I get back?"

"That's fine, whatever you decide." He confidently smiled as he helped her into the car making certain to not let her know that he was interested in her. He was cool, and aloof, not what Asia was used to.

"Okay Spencer." Asia reached out the window to shake his hand, "it was a pleasure meeting you." Asia waved as she drove off. When she was far enough away she exhaled "What a weirdo." Asia explained how everything he was into, she was not and everything she was into he was not. "And he was talking about his fucking mother, like; I'm ever going to meet the woman that raised him, give me a break!"

Cymone laughed, "hey Asia, let's go to the mall and do some shopping for our trip."

Asia and Cymone headed to Willowbrook Mall hoping to catch some cruise wear.

The lot was so crowded they could not find a space. "Let's go to Short Hills Mall, they have valet parking there." Asia sighed as she pulled out of the lot.

◆

Asia was awakened by the tide rising and touching her bottom through the chaise she lounged on, on the beach. She slowly opened her eyes, awaking from a deep sleep, all she could think about how happy she was to be away from the bustle of everyone at home, giving into the commercialism and hype of Christmas. She looked to her left and to her right and saw nothing but miles of beach; it was just she and the gorgeous hues of the purple and orange sunset. Instantly she felt spiritually connected, balanced and centered, it was only right to appeal to her goddess. *I know that I have been blessed many times over, but I would be remiss if I blew this opportunity to thank you for all that I have been given, and to let you know that I think I am ready, I am ready to join my life with someone and make a significant contribution to this world. Please guide me to the correct one.* And with that she rose from the chaise, gathered her belongings and headed back to her suite.

Asia walked in to the suite to find Cymone humming to "The Things you do for Love" By 10CC, the natives just loved older American pop music. She was sipping wine and about to heat up left over dinner from the night before. "Hey girl, where you been?" Cymone took another deep sip.

"Hey hun, I fell asleep on the chaise lounge on the beach. Girl the tide came in and a wave caught my ass, I thought I peed on myself! Let me get some of that wine.

"So what do you want to do tonight?" Cymone was slurring a bit but her eyes were glistening like a child on Christmas morning.

"Well let's go into town and see if any of my old friends are here."

Much to Asia's surprise, Aruba had become quite the couples spot, and Cymone was not exactly her type. Asia was impressed with how developed the downtown area had become, she loved the new mall with the waterway in the center, *how ingenious* she thought!

Asia and Cymone chose a bar right in town to begin their night of debauchery.

As they sipped martini's Asia told Cymone of a fling she had with a police officer from the island when she was in college.

Cymone was intrigued by the story and figured it would be worth investigating to see if they can locate Asia's fling.

"Cymone, you can't be serious." Asia shrieked. "You really want to try to find the police station and Elsio?"

"Fuck yeah, look girl we need to liven up this night, too many couples around here, besides, where one cop works, so do others, I would assume there is a plethora of men for me to choose from."

Asia laughed at Cymone and could hardly argue with her reasoning. "Okay, I think I remember how to get to the police department, let's go." They paid for their drinks and slithered off of their respective bar stools.

Asia pulled Cymone along the dark street, dimly lit only by the moon and the two streetlights at the end of the block. The clicking of their heels was so pronounced it echoed. They stopped before a nondescript brick building. Asia sighed deeply "this is crazy."

"That's what I was thinking in the bar, but you wanted to come. We are here, and there is no way we are turning back now." Cymone reached out to fluff up Asia's hair and continued, "you look gorgeous, and we are going to have some fun, so fuck that, get your ass in there and find this man you have been telling me about and see if after all these years there is still a spark."

Asia nervously smiled and smoothed her hands down her back side, and confidently proceeded up the stairs of the police station.

As they walked in, the fluorescent light forced them to squint, they approached the plastic window, behind it was a uniformed officer, middle aged, chunky and hardly up to what Cymone was expecting in the land of beautiful men.

"Excuse me" Asia mumbled.

Cymone pushed her to the side, "Hello there." She offered a wide smile and a seductive voice, the dispatcher glanced up, his eyes slowly tilted up Cymone's body and finally locked with hers.

"Yes ma'am?"

Makin' Happy

"Hi I am from the states and looking to find a friend of mine, he is an officer, his name is Elsio, and do you know him?"

"Yeah I know him. You a friend of his"

"Well yes, sort of, we have not seen each other in years."

The officer stood up and looked at Cymone then back at Asia, "What's your name?"

"Asia, Asia Blake, from New Jersey"

"I will be right back." He smirked at Cymone and she gave him a sultry smile. He walked to the door behind him, pressed a code on the keypad and entered.

"Well now, that was easy." Cymone sighed. "I never did a chunky cop before but the more I drink I think the better men look around here."

"Girl you are crazy."

The chunky cop emerged from "the back room" and told us to have a seat. He motioned to the benches across from the window.

Cymone and Asia walked to the vinyl bench and sat. Asia began to get uncomfortable, as Cymone played eye flirting with the chunky cop behind the window.

"Hey Cy, you got a smoke?"

"Yeah let's go outside and have one" as Cymone spoke she flirted with the caged cop who was practically drooling on himself.

They headed outside and lit up a smoke, suddenly, a police car came flying from around the dark corner and up the street with lights flashing. Asia and Cymone stopped in their tracks shocked when a spot light appeared on them.

A tall slender native in full uniform exited the vehicle and yelled "hold it right there."

Asia shrieked "Elsio!" She ran to the car and gave him a big hug and kiss. Cymone took a drag from her cigarette and smiled.

"Well, well pretty lady you have not changed a bit, what has it been five, six years?" Elsio flashed his winning smile from beneath his thick and well-manicured mustache.

"It has been way too long. You're still tall and sexy I see"

He blushed

Asia continued, "Allow me to introduce you to one of my dearest friends. She put her arm through his and walked him over to where Cymone had been smoking. "Elsio, this is Cymone, Cymone, Elsio.

"You can't have all the ladies for yourself", blared a voice from Elsio's radio.

Elsio grabbed the radio and pressed down a button "Don't worry Charlie; I can't handle both, what's your twenty?" Elsio looked at Asia and Cymone and smiled "news of attractive visitors travels fast here. My buddy Charlie is on his way to meet the lovely Cymone he heard about from Bob the dispatcher."

Cymone brushed her hair back behind one ear and smiled. Charlie pulled up on a motorcycle, right behind Elsio's cruiser. He hopped off the bike and made his way to Cymone. He was slender and sexy, with deep beautiful eyes, exactly Cymone's type.

Asia and Cymone went back to the bar and waited for Charlie and Elsio to get off from their shift and shower. The night was splendid, a trip to the Casino, a late night dinner at the Indian Rock Garden, a place where only island natives and the ultra lucky visitors attend. It's an all night restaurant, bar and club. When approaching it, it looks like a mountain; all you see are cars, no signs, not one bit evidence of the treasure that waits behind the guarded doors. Upon entering it is like walking into a luxury hide away. It is a space created in the base of a mountain, with rock walls and waterfalls, a plethora of plush seats that are the size of beds amassed with sensuous silk pillows and a thumping beat blaring from the speakers. Exotically beautiful dancers in cages and the most beautiful food servers, both the male and female servers looked like models.

Asia's eyes were wide, she felt like she was in paradise. Elsio and Charlie whisked Asia and Cymone through the club, people whispered as the crowed parted for them. Elsio led them to a roped off section that was for VIP's. They felt like celebrities.

Charlie asked Cymone to dance and whisked her away on the dance floor.

Elsio and Asia snuggled up on one of the bed like sofas, a bottle of Champagne was brought to their table by a server who looked like a caramel colored Fabio, and he opened the bottle and poured their drinks. Elsio handed a glass to Asia, whispered to something in the food server's ear, he nodded and he was gone. Fabio later returned with a platter of the most exquisite food, fresh fruits, and huge shrimp with an array of sauces for dipping, lobster tails and drawn butter. Elsio motioned to Asia to just lean back and relax. He rolled up his sleeves "Let me take care of you princess"

He said as he fed her.

Asia awoke with Elsio laying beside her naked in a deep sleep. She looked around the unfamiliar surroundings. They were in a hotel room, overlooking the ocean, the wall that faced the water was entirely glass and every window was open creating the white window sheers to blow fiercely into the room. She pulled herself up from the bed and wrapped a sheet around her naked body; her hair was askew framing her lovely brown face. She walked to the door leading to the patio. She wondered how Elsio could afford such extravagance. *On a cops salary?* She made a mental note to ask him what was going on. She sat on one of the chairs on the patio and looked out onto the blue ocean, tranquil and lovely, with the sun glistening off of it.

Elsio quietly walked up behind her and placed his hands on her shoulders, then slid them down to her breasts and kissed the top of her head. "Good morning Princess."

She leaned her head back to kiss him on his lips. "Good morning sexy."

"You are still the most passionate incredible woman I have ever had the pleasure of tasting. You are still exquisite, like a fine wine you are only getting better with age."

Asia blushed. "Thank you Elsio." She paused for a moment. "I have been meaning to ask you something." She grabbed his hand and led him to sit beside her.

"Ask away princess."

As she opened her mouth to speak, there was a gentle knock on the door, it was room service carting in another spectacular platter of food, fresh squeezed juices and coffee. Elsio loved to eat and knew how to have whatever he wanted brought to him quickly.

He smiled and bit into a mango slice, the juice was running down his chin. Asia walked up to him and licked the juice from his chin and worked her way to his lips and kissed him.

She began to kiss and lick his ear. "We need to talk baby."

He pulled away and led her to the bed. "We will talk after I taste you again." In one fell swoop he was between her legs licking her clit exactly the way she loved. She moaned.

He jumped up and grabbed the platter of fruit and brought it back to bed. He began to create his own dish Asia a la mode. He placed fruit and berries on her belly and sprinkled ambrosia on her breasts. Asia shivered from the chill. She delighted in watching Elsio feast away on her. His mouth was incredible. He licked and sucked her from head to toe. He was incredibly sensuous, and no one had ever sucked her toes like Elsio. He worshiped Asia's lovely feet as he did the rest of her body.

She melted with every lick. She rolled over and reached for the ambrosia. She made an ambrosia sundae on his throbbing dick. She hungrily consumed every inch of him. Oral sex and food, were her favorites.

When she completed her heavenly act and had him convulsing with pleasure, she reached over him and grabbed one of his cigarettes. He rubbed her curly mound of hair and spoke with his heavy Dutch accent, "You are so lovely, honestly Asia."

"Thank you darling. Now tell me, what is going on with you?"

"What do you want to know?" He tucked both of his hands behind his head and looked deeply into her eyes. "For you, I am an open book."

"Elsio, how can you afford all of this? Last time I saw you, you were struggling. Unless the police department paid huge bonuses."

"Asia, the Indian Rock Garden is mine, I am part owner" he hesitated, "my wife owns the other half."

Asia was in shock, she immediately pulled his hand from behind his head, no ring. "Elsio, how could you not tell me?"

"You did not ask my sweet, until now and I am telling you. Does it make that much of a difference?"

"I think you know the answer to that." Asia got up and wrapped the sheet around her with the cigarette hanging out of her mouth. She stepped back out onto the balcony and walked over to the railing and looked out onto the ocean. She really was not sure of what to feel. She knew that she wanted someone in her life, but not Elsio, he was her holiday lover. It had been years since they have seen each other, and she certainly did not ask what his status was because the painful reality was that it did not matter. Then she realized that if he and his status did not matter much to her, she did not matter much to him either and the feeling left her pretty cold. At that moment she realized that being alone was a hell of a lot better than being with someone who really did not give a shit.

She thought of lighting into him, but how could she? He was completely honest with her, painfully so. She wanted to ask so many questions, the how could he? Why did he? Who was she? And how could he disrespect her like that in the club? Asia continued to smoke her cigarette in silence. As she exhaled she reflected on an article that she had read in a magazine on the plane. It was about marriage and the fact that it was just a contract, with terms and everyone's term was different. She realized that this was a harsh reality; most people like her grew up with some unrealistic, idealistic vision of how marriage should be. Then she recalled the conversation with her mother where she was shocked to discover that Rebecca's idea of happiness was far from being married to William and having Asia and Josh.

Elsio came up behind her, gently placing his hands on Asia's arms. He nestled his chin on her shoulder. "Are you ok my sweet?"

She reached up and ran her fingers through his hair and gently down his face, never taking her eyes off the ocean.

"I am just fine." She lied.

Asia arrived back at the suite to find Cymone a bit worried, yet smitten with Charlie. The last few days of their vacation was spent together on the beach every morning, shopping in the afternoon, spa every evening, and lavish dinners with Elsio and Charlie at the Indian Rock Garden at night. Asia never approached the subject of Elsio's wife, all he did share was that she was in Holland and she was the daughter of a wealthy Dutch government official.

As Asia and Cymone deplaned, she took a deep sigh of relief. She was able to discuss the entire situation with Cymone without judgment. Cymone had a clear don't ask don't tell policy with Charlie and it served them well all week. It was a perfect single girl's escape to the islands. Every girl needs to have it at least once in her lifetime.

Asia got home to a mound of messages and holiday cards and well wishes. She was due back into the station for the New Years Eve broadcast that was her arrangement with the manager since she was given the week off after Christmas.

CHAPTER TEN

Mystify Me

I NEED PERFECTION, SOME TWISTED SELECTION
THAT TANGLES ME TO KEEP ME ALIVE

Yeva excitedly welcomed a cranky yet stunningly sun kissed Asia back to work. "Welcome back sunshine." Yeva was way to chipper on New Year's Eve. "How was your trip? Might I say that you look fabulous?"

"Thank you baby, this just sucks, I would much rather be home and in bed. My trip was fantastic, I wish it was seven or nine days instead of five, but here I am."

Asia filled up her water bottle at the cooler and made a cup of coffee, her pre show ritual. She sat down in her studio and put her headphones on. Yeva motioned to her to switch to the intercom through the glass.

Asia shrugged in frustration, she needed to review some notes before she went on. She flicked on the intercom. "Yes Yeva what is it?"

Yeva excitedly spoke, "I just had to tell you, Spencer is down for the holidays, and he kept asking about you, so I invited him over for the show tonight, figured once we wrapped, me you Spencer and Celeste could go play pool, grab a beer or something."

Asia had a *what the fuck?* expression on her face. She was cranky; she thought how she was smitten with Jake and smooching with him a year ago, now she is working post affair with yet another married man in another country. "Ok, one beer then I am out."

"Excellent and you're on in fifteen." Yeva smiled and clicked off the intercom.

Asia's show went unbelievably swiftly. Celeste and Spencer showed up with bottles of Gloria Ferrer champagne, and a delicious meal of chicken wings and potato salad. Asia left her car in the studio's garage and went back to Montclair with Spencer, Celeste and Yeva. They decided the party they created in the studio was enough. Spencer was staying in the guesthouse, which was a lovely one-bedroom studio with a fireplace. He built a fire as Asia rambled on about how champagne makes her tipsy.

They proceeded to sit and talk for hours about family, school, and life. Asia was pleasantly surprised that Spencer and she did have more things in common. He was sweet, hung onto her every word and was very attentive. He asked her if he could kiss her. He gently showered her with wonderful kisses and affection.

Spencer shared with Asia stories about his family, his plight to obtain his two masters degrees with little assistance from his family. He was the middle child and though he had more degrees than his brothers and sister, he was the greatest disappointment to his mother, for being a musician was hardly serious enough to please her. His youngest brother was a judge and his older brother was in IT and his sister was a nurse.

Asia was impressed that such productive members emerged from his family and though he presented his mother as "different". Asia felt she clearly had a handle on raising kids, since they all had impressive levels of education and interesting careers.

Asia drifted off to awaken on the sofa with her feet nestled in Spencer's lap. The both drifted off as he massaged her feet. The fire was ablaze and she felt warm, cozy, and connected. As he slept he looked so happy and to Asia, she felt significant, finally she felt like she was meaningful to someone. Then and there she decided he could be something important to her. She smiled and nestled under the blanket and went back to sleep.

Spencer gently nudged Asia to awaken her. He smiled an awkward smile. "Would you like to get some breakfast?"

"That would be lovely." She said sleepily. She felt comfortable with Spencer. After their long talk, she liked the way he looked on paper. After all, thirty was creeping around the corner and she placed unnecessary pressure to do as her friends and family were doing. Faced with the fear of a fate like Sam's and the lavishness of a happy married home life that Yeva, Celeste, Lance, and Charla had was looking awfully appealing, especially after her trip to Aruba and getting an unsettling glimpse at marriage from Elsio's relationship.

Asia asked to use Spencer's phone to call Yeva, she wanted to make sure that she and Celeste were awake before she barged in on them asking for clothes to change into. Spencer told her there was no need. He had something she could borrow. He led her to the bathroom and handed her a terry cloth robe. "Beneath the sink are spare tooth brushes, towels, and everything you would need to shower. I will pull some of my sweat pants and a shirt for you to throw on if you don't mind."

Asia smiled, "thank you Spencer that will be fine."

When Asia emerged from the bathroom in her robe, she found lying on the bed was a University of Maine sweatshirt with matching pants. She got dressed and entered the living area to find Spencer in the kitchen. He had raided Celeste's and Yeva's fridge and began creating a delicious platter of fruit, brie cheese, crackers, mini bagels with lox and cream cheese, coffee was percolating and it filled the space with such a warm cozy feeling. Asia felt right at home. She sat on the sofa before the roaring fire and watched Spencer in the kitchen, not only was she impressed but she was smitten.

Spencer placed the platter of delicious treats before her, "I hope there is something on here you like."

"Yum, I think I like it all, thank you." He sat down beside her and asked if he could kiss her. Asia said yes. They kissed. It was not fireworks and rockets, but it was sweet and warm. Asia decided she cared deeply for him.

They sat all morning by the fire and talked about their unsuccessful turns at relationships. Spencer was thirty-four and a serial monogamist, he was ready to move onto the next phase of his life. The recipe can be amazingly sweet or terribly disastrous when you mix two people who are simply tired of their current situations.

Asia figured they were doing well after all they looked great on paper. They continued to share and laugh. Spencer suddenly took a serious tone; he took her hand and placed it on his heart, "Tell me a secret, something you have not shared with someone else."

Asia squinted her eyes and thought for a moment. "Okay, my mom has this big issue with my dad. She thinks that he has a tendency to be nicer to other people's children than he was to us."

"Do you believe he was?"

"Sometimes, but my dad is a gregarious dude, he could be salty and toss some zingers at home and many of his customers never saw that side of him. He may have been nicer in distant dealings, but he bought all of my cars and even named his business after me, I hardly think he has placed anyone else's child before me."

"Your turn." Asia stated.

"One time my mother was behaving so horribly, my father had to smack the shit out of her in front of a group of people."

"Oh my, was there a history of violence between them?"

"No that was the first and last time he put his hands on her ever. She was verbally abusive, and she was drunk, she had revealed a nasty secret about a friend over a card game, when she would not heed to warnings to shut up, my dad smacked her so hard across the mouth she fell back in her chair and everyone just laughed."

Asia and Spencer began to laugh.

Their relationship progressed. Spencer put in for a leave that semester to pick up teaching classes in New York. He stayed in his mother's Apartment in Harlem, and he and Asia stole away as many moments as possible. They were inseparable. He was like an addiction for her. She felt the need to be with him constantly and he needed to know her every move. He would often be waiting for her when she completed shifts at the station and they would have late night dates. Asia spent little to no time writing and saw her friends and family less. On their second week of dating, Spencer proposed to Asia, sans a ring. He claimed to not be materialistic, that he would much rather spend that kind of money on a piano and he had his eye on a seven thousand dollar Korg keyboard. Asia was so smitten, engrossed in the love, she did not even care. She was crazy for him and was willing to have him any way possible.

A training session offered by a leading maker of computerized music technology was offered in Arizona. Spencer wanted to go, he was making little money and when he approached Asia with his desire to attend, he presented her being the reason for him taking the leave and not having the money. He asked her to borrow her credit card to attend the conference. "Celeste works for the hotel chain that is hosting the conference, so I know I can get a room pretty inexpensively." He moaned to Asia like a child. Asia knew it was not a wise decision, but feeling guilty and in love she handed it over to pay for his stay at a hotel.

Once the bill came in Asia found out that he stayed at top of the line hotel several miles from the conference and partook in spa treatments while he was there.

She felt betrayed. When she approached him about it, he was cold and distant. His attitude was that of him being entitled to do as he wished after all he assured her that he would pay her back and that it was discounted because of Celeste's connection. Asia foolishly understood his argument, and figured if she had the opportunity to stay at a $300 a night hotel for $60, she would have done it as well.

She loved him and she felt like she had an investment in a relationship now. She tolerated his attitude and accepted his flights of entitlement.

Now it was spring and after a marathon Sunday of lovemaking, Asia proposed that Spencer move in with her. He managed to agree but ascertaining that he would have no financial responsibility, since he left his job to be with her. She agreed.

And so the downward spiral began. The more he wanted the more Asia gave. This behavior was completely out of character for her. She was not the type of woman to completely devote herself to a man but she slowly became that woman. She slowly began to mold into him. Asia was swept up in the fantasy of the brilliant musician becoming inspired by her essence and beauty. She wanted him to be awe struck by her the same way she was in awe of him. The only thing Spencer was struck by the wondrous fan he had in Asia. She provided him with a lifestyle he felt he was entitled to and she constantly praised him.

Spencer's former lovers were all musicians. So to them his musical ability was looked upon as mediocre at best. He would always speak of how his former lovers and friends who are musicians were jealous of him and his talent. To Asia he was the best. Every time he sat at the piano to play, she would simply freeze and assume a trance like state. His music seduced her mind to drop everything and report to him. It was hauntingly reminiscent of Svengali's power over Trilby. And now, he was to become her husband.

Asia had conflicting thoughts of what her fantasies detailed and the reality of her situation. She had always dreamed of ceremonial grandeur when the man she would spend the rest of her life with asked for her hand in marriage. An elegant ring symbolizing his love would accent the perfect proposal; of course he would have dragged Rebecca to the finest jeweler to assist in the selection. Asia never viewed this dream as materialistic, just a fact of life.

Makin' Happy

You grow up, you go to college, you get a job, you get a guy, you get the ring, and you get married. Basic steps leading to a simple life, a plan that everyone seemed to follow, everyone except Spencer.

Spencer was so dead set against buying Asia a ring it infuriated Rebecca. This only solidified a tense discussion Asia had with her family back when she was in high school. William, Rebecca, Asia and Josh were dining at their favorite steak house and Asia was admiring her mother's four-carat Round Brilliant perfect stone. Asia slipped the ring onto her finger and held up her hand to marvel at its brilliance. As she was lost in the fantasy of having one of her own, William blurted out, "yeah get a good long look at what you will never have."

Enter the speeding automobile skid to a huge crash sound that resonated in Asia's head. Asia and Rebecca were in utter shock. Josh looked at Asia with a "that's fucked up" expression all over his face.

"William, why would you say such a thing?" Rebecca quipped.

"Because it is true. No sense in setting her up to believe that she will get a rock like that. Plain and simple." William proceeded to cut and eat his steak as if nothing was wrong.

Asia was crushed, but never would she broach the subject with her father again. She made up her mind that he really felt he was part of a dying breed of black men, who spoiled their black wives, those men were few and far between and William and Asia knew it.

The reality was she was not skinny, fair skinned and she was intelligent with the credentials to back it up, not exactly the top ten things on a black man's wish list. Though Asia was beautiful, she had a look that was unique and all her own, hardly the size 8 trophy arm candy. Now here she sits, engaged to a man her father despises, because in William's mind, Spencer could not carry the jock straps of the class of men to which William belonged. For

William it had less to do with providing material things to his daughter. He could see that Asia cared far more for him than he did her and it pained him so.

Asia and Spencer had taken a day off to lie around in bed. He had been living with her for a few months now and she was thrilled. Asia adopted a feeling of *him and me against the world*. She had not seen or spoken with Cymone, Lance and Charla in months. Because of the tension rising between her family and Spencer, she rarely went home for Sunday dinners.

Spencer kissed her, "Let's go to City Hall and do it Asia. Let's get married today."

Intoxicated by love and fantasy, Asia agreed. As they stood before City Hall, Spencer got down on one knee. Asia began to cry. He professed his love for her. He shared with her how his life has improved since they met. He took her hand and placed it on his heart. "Will you be my wife?" Asia hugged and kissed him. Not even concerned by this being his second proposal to her and still no ring.

"Yes, Spencer Barksdale, I will be your wife." She happily kissed him.

On the ride home, Asia reflected on the many conversations they had where Spencer would always end the discussion with "I thought you were different from those materialistic gold diggers and that's why I chose you. What kind of woman needs a symbol, a ring, to override a man's word?" Asia heard it so many times she began to believe it. It was like she was hypnotized. His crusade became hers; she was on her soapbox that women who demanded rings were materialistic.

Asia was certainly educated and smart, but when it came to Spencer it was like her brain was on disconnect. She was beyond in love with him; she was in sheer awe of him. His talent, his power, his ability to control every situation, and his ability to be comfortable being cruel made Asia a loyal subject. Spencer took great pride in disturbing the psyche of those he was connected to. A craft he learned from his mother, and perfected on his own.

Mavis Barksdale was the meanest, harshest woman Asia had ever met. She would spit cruelty like a snake spits venom. Yet she had many people who worshipped her, at Christmas time her house would be filled to the rim with gifts, cards and food from adoring fans and followers, how could they be friends? They hardly were treated with kindness and compassion. She raised her children in the same fashion. The nastier she was, the more they did for her.

The months that followed her secret wedding flew by. Christmas time was approaching and Asia felt joy. She felt secure and a sense of warmth. She had her husband, and she was determined to be his muse. She would watch him spend countless hours in his cage, the term she dubbed for being behind his racks of keyboards. She would hope that one day he would emerge from behind the cage to share with her a song he had written just for her. As she sat and watched him, she realized she had not written anything in months, almost a year. She convinced herself that the source of her writing was from her pain and longing for love, now that she had it, she was complete.

Asia shifted to the morning drive show so that she could spend her evenings with Spencer. This also made her less sought after for late nightclub appearances, which Spencer was not too thrilled with anyway. She pushed on with her shifts, after all someone had to make money and provide them with benefits. In her mind she was supporting a musician who was gifted and was soon to make it. Never recognizing that Spencer had no desire to make it, he could care less if he played publicly again. He was happy with his adjunct positions at some of the local colleges. It gave him a reason to get out and share his brilliance.

One Sunday morning Spencer was in his cage and Asia was dutifully watching him; he emerged to announce he was hungry. "I am going to make breakfast."

Asia bounced to the kitchen like a love struck puppy, "what can I do to help?"

"How about cutting up the potatoes, I am going to make some hash browns." He handed her the colander with the washed potatoes, a cutting board and a Henkels knife he pulled from his from his knife kit in the pantry. "Nice small pieces babe." He demanded.

She nodded and walked over to the table. She placed down the cutting board and the potatoes. She sliced into the potato and the scent immediately brought on a wave of nausea that sent her running to the bathroom and to her surprise she threw up. Spencer followed her and stood behind her in the door way.

"Are you ok?" he asked.

"I feel really sick all of a sudden," then she began to throw up even more, "I wonder if I have a virus or something." She made her way back to bed as Spencer cooked. A rush of horror came over her when she realized that her period was three days late.

Cymone and Timmy were coming over for dinner later that Sunday evening and it was the first time Asia had seen her months. She did not want to cancel and was determined to go through with dinner. Spencer and Asia headed to the market to pick up necessities for the dinner party. Asia headed to the health and beauty isle and Spencer made a b line for the seafood. He was intending on steaming a bass for dinner. Asia headed towards him and dropped a pregnancy test kit in the cart.

"What's that for?" Spencer's tone was a bit harsh.

"What do you think?" Asia said smartly. She started to feel dizzy. She grabbed her stomach and held onto Spencer, "I don't feel so good, the smells, they are making me sick, I will meet you in the car."

Makin' Happy

After vomiting in the trashcan in the parking lot, Asia made it safely to the car. She put her head back and closed her eyes. She began to envision the image of her dancing on the beach with a little girl in her harms, both of them with hair blowing in the summer wind and laughing. Then she became afraid, how could she have a baby? Then she remembered, she was married now, suddenly all was ok.

Spencer broke her pleasant daydream with opening the trunk to place the groceries in. He climbed into the driver's seat, turned the key to start up the car and turned to Asia. "Should you be pregnant, I certainly hope you are not thinking about keeping it."

Asia was crushed. How dare he speak to her that way? She said nothing; she just put her head back and placed her hand over her eyes. When they arrived to the loft, Asia said nothing. Her heart was breaking. On the elevator ride up from the garage he broke the silence. "Look, I am not ready to have a kid. I thought you wanted to wait till you were in your mid thirties, I thought that was what we agreed upon."

"Well Spencer, nature has a funny way of intervening on your grand scheme. If I was pregnant, what would be so wrong with that?

"A lot would be wrong with it." He paused and took a deep breath and spoke in a terse tone "it is not what I wanted for us right now."

"Spencer, if I am pregnant we can continue this bullshit conversation then. For the record, if I am and this test is positive, there is no way I am *not* having this baby." The elevator opened and she stepped off leaving him there to carry the groceries alone.

Once he arrived into the loft she took the kit and went right into the bathroom, he unpacked groceries, not phased in the slightest by her comment or actions.

While in the bathroom she cried as she took the test. She cried harder as she waited for the result. For this supposed happy time she was terribly sad. She was married, and according to the stick, she was with child and she never felt so alone in her entire life.

This battle Asia won, she announced to Spencer that she confirmed her pregnancy. He never mentioned not wanting a child again.

Eight months later Asia gave birth to a beautiful baby girl, Zoe. According to general theory, her life was complete. She had her husband, and a healthy baby. She continued to feel empty and her post partum depression did not help. She often had conversations with herself asking who she was. She had nightmares of her individuality slipping out of her hands, she was a wife, and a mother those had become the defining factors and she was not happy with that.

Suddenly Asia was like a single mother, she drove into the city, dropping Zoe off at the sitter on her way, after every show she would bundle up Zoe and collect her and schlep back to Jersey. Spencer was too busy picking up random classes and composing at all hours to concern himself with the labors of parenting. He managed to miss dinners together and arrive just as Zoe was put to bed. He never wanted to do anything together unless it surrounded his favorite things, his friends, music, or fishing. It had gotten to the point that he would completely ignore Asia. He would come in from work, she would say hello or greet him with a kiss and he would stand there, non responsive, or continue to walk by her and go about his things never saying a word to her.

By the time Zoe was two, she and Asia were in such a rhythm it was becoming obvious to Asia that Spencer wanted no part of being in a family. Asia began to see a therapist once she hit what she felt like was bottom. One day she took Zoe to the sitter, cancelled her show and went home. She smoked weed and cried all day. That was her bottom. The voices in her head were telling her Spencer's words that everything that went wrong in the relationship was her fault. She phoned and then met with a therapist who helped Asia see that the errors in the relationship were not all her fault but she had to accept responsibility for the poor choices she made. He also gave Asia paperwork on Narcissistic Personality Disorder and encouraged her to read it.

Asia poured over it line by line in utter shock how Spencer completely fit the profile. From his relationship with his less than stable mother who thought telling him she "shit him out" and that he was a "no good black motherfucker" were a terms of endearment. Asia studied the pages given to her. She used it as sort of bedside reading. Spencer was so unconcerned with what she did, he never noticed. He had become so curt with her and what little affection he demonstrated earlier in the relationship was out the window.

One Saturday afternoon Asia and Zoe were napping. She was half awake; gently stroking Zoe's curly hair and marveling at the joy she brought to Asia. Asia then tied to reflect on how many meals they had eaten together as a family in the past three months, she could not recall one. Her therapist pointed out that was a problem. Zoe was awakened by Spencer allowing the door to slam as he entered the loft, she peeked up at Asia and smiled, then she ran to Spencer chanting "Daddy, daddy" with her arms flailing.

He stopped in mid step as she wrapped her arms around his legs. He said nothing to her, he just stood there and looked down at her and waited for her to loosen her grip. Once she let go he walked by her like she was not there. He headed straight for the cage and threw on his headphones. Zoe began to cry and ran back to Asia and hopped on the bed. She rocked and cried, Asia scooped her up and pulled her on top of her, stroking Zoë's head whispering mommy loves you baby, and rocking on the bed.

Asia asked Zoe, "You want to go visit grandma and pop-pop sweetie?"

Zoe was excited "yeah mommy let's go!"

Asia went into Zoë's room, shoved a few clothes and clean panties in a bag, grabbed her purse and left the loft without saying a word to Spencer. She phoned her mother on the cell phone and asked if she would keep Zoe for the evening.

"Bring me my baby" was Rebecca's response. Rebecca was infuriated by Asia and Spencer's relationship but Zoe was the most spectacular precious gem to come out of such a fucked up relationship.

Once Asia got Zoe nestled in the family room playpen, Rebecca walked Asia out to her car. "Are you growing tired of being a Stepford Wife?" Rebecca said in a sarcastic tone. Her relationship with Rebecca was strained and fragile, but she knew Rebecca would be her rock; she just had to roll with the salty punches such as this one.

"Mom, he has fucked with me, that's ok, I am getting through it, but I will be damned, before I let him fuck with my baby."

"What did he do? You know I always thought he tortured her."

"Yes mom I know." Asia nodded as Rebecca recounted observing Spencer taking sheer joy in making Zoe cry just by uttering her name. It was his sort of horse and pony show.

When Asia returned to the loft, Spencer was still in headphones in his cage, he did not notice that they were gone. Asia walked over to him and motioned that they need to talk. She attempted to have a heart to heart with him they were always such a challenge. Every attempt to discuss her unhappiness only provided Spencer with the platform to invalidate her feelings. Through the years, each conversation ended with Asia whisking off to smoke a bowl to numb her sadness. Not this time, she had an amazing sense of clarity, since she had not smoked in months since she started therapy. Spencer was not ready for what she threw at him.

He sat on the bed and looked at her with his haughty "you don't know what you're talking about" posture. She handed him the paperwork that her therapist gave her. He glanced through all thirty some-odd -highlighted pages. He looked at her and said, "Yes, so?"

"Spencer I think you have a problem, I am willing to help you with it. Perhaps we should do therapy together."

He chuckled, "No way, I am not crazy; you're the one with the problems and issues Asia, not me."

Asia walked to the fridge to get a glass of water and to cool down from his snide remark. She knew that counting from ten would be better than ripping his head off. She noticed a thank you card on the kitchen counter. She read the card and it was thanking Spencer for the gift, the handwriting appeared to be that of a young person. Asia walked back to the bedroom with the card in hand, "What's this?"

"It is a card from Lorraine's son; he was thanking me for the birthday gift I got him."

Asia's mind did a scan, Lorraine? Oh yes, his co-worker, Lorraine. A woman who Spencer had become close to and often called the house, even at inappropriate hours. When Asia met her she was shocked to find that Lorraine was short, dowdy and though she had a sweet face, was hardly attractive. Asia did recall she resembled one of Spencer's former girlfriends.

"Well that was nice." She said calmly.

Rage hit Asia like a bolt of lightning. In the years they had been together, Spencer never bought her anything for her birthday nor did Mr. Not Materialistic ever buy anything for Zoe. "What the fuck are you doing purchasing gifts for someone else's child and you don't even do shit for your own?"

"Oh Asia please, once again you are thinking about things, I am so tired of your bullshit, besides, don't go confusing me with your father, he was the one you have the issue with about treating other kids better, am I right?"

She wanted to slap him, but he was bigger, much bigger and she knew violence was not the way to solve anything. Asia just cringed at what he said. How dare he bring up her secret about her father? That was just downright dirty.

"You know Spencer; I don't even know who you are anymore. You clearly are sharing your hopes and dreams with someone else. So why do you even bother?"

"Asia, I don't have a desire to share anything with you. I don't know why I bother. Asia, I do not want to be married anymore."

Asia was stunned but relieved at the same time. She felt the weight of the world was off of her shoulders.

All she could say in response was "Good, I don't want to be married either."

And just like that he was gone. Spencer had removed all of his belongings before Zoe arrived home that next evening.

Asia took Zoe to the Vineyard to open the house. As they cruised up route 95 with the top down on Asia's Jeep, Zoe called from the back "Hey mom turn on the radio. There was Asia's song, Crystal Waters crooning *Makin' Happy*. Zoe chimed in

"Ah ooh-wee ooh, ooh-wee ooh, ooh-wee, ooh-wee, ooh-wee, just making happy making happy, happy, happy, happy."

Asia welled up with tears, "Sing it baby" she shouted as she pumped her fist in the air.

Asia's cell phone rang, "Hello"

"Yo, slow down, this hardly a club, turn that damn music down!"

Asia reached up to look in her rearview mirror, as she looked beyond Zoe, she saw Cymone laughing on the cell phone, and she was closely following behind. Cymone had in tow Brianna and two of her friends from school. Following Cymone's car was Lance and Charla and their son Sam.

ABOUT THE AUTHOR

Niki Kendall is an educator, filmmaker, lecturer, motivational speaker, event planner and the author of several published articles and short stories.

A graduate of Rutgers University Mason Gross School of the Arts (MFA) and Montclair State University (BA), she was born and raised in New Jersey and currently works in public education.

Niki serves on various committees within her community and volunteers her time writing grants and doing web design. She loves to cook and entertain for friends and family. She resides in Apex, North Carolina with her talented artist/musician daughter.

Printed in the United States
141353LV00004B/8/P

9 781438 952185